THROUGH A
PASSAGE IN TIME

Fred Hale

Through a Passage in Time
Copyright 2021 by Fred Hale

ISBN-13: Paperback 978-1-952648-38-0
ISBN-13: EPub 978-1-952648-39-7

Because of the dynamic nature of the Internet, any web addresses or links contained in this book may have changed since publication and may no longer be valid. The views expressed in this work are solely those of the author and do not necessarily reflect the views of the publisher, and the publisher hereby disclaims any responsibility for them.

Printed in the United States of America

To order additional copies of this book.
Contact Haynes Media
1-844-828-0428
www.haynesmediagroup.com

My name is Matthew H. Stein. I was a college professor at a local University. I taught world history for several years there until I retired. I never married and I'm still a single man at the age of seventy-two. I stand six foot four inches and have a yellow lab named Buck. He is my best friend. It is November 2nd the air is crisp; the breeze is gentle. I am strolling on a morning walk with Buck as I try to do every day. Though my mind is on things that happened a week ago, I can't help but notice a low-lying fog settling in as I am crossing a bridge on the river near my home. I stop to watch the water flow by, and slowly I look downriver as the fog seems to cover it like a soft blanket. The events of a week ago just won't leave my mind and I start to daydream about things that are inexplicable to me.

One week ago, I was watching a news broadcast about a treasure-seeking ship. Treasure hunters were looking for a sunken vessel that is supposed to be off the shore's northeast of Venezuela. It is a small chain of islands known as the Grenadines. The island is known as St. Lucia. The ship is supposed to be inside the Port of Castries with its cargo intact. As I was watching the broadcast I knew just as sure as I am sitting here that they are looking in the wrong place. I have an eerie feeling that I know where this sunken ship is located. I listened with intensity for the name of the ship that they are looking for. . ..

Someone said they thought it may possibly be the *Shark*.

I don't know why, nor do I understand how, but I am sure I know where the vessel is. I just know they are looking in the wrong area.

Jumping up to get my world map to look to see where they are. I chuckled to myself and looked down at Buck. "I know where the *Shark* is,"

I told him. "Latitude 12° north, longitude 61° west, depth approximately one hundred feet. It is about two to three miles southeast of Palm Island."

In years past I had often felt that I didn't belong in this time, that I was truly someone else. I understood even at a very early age that I belonged in another era. I never really told anyone but kept this to myself. As I was deep in thought, flashbacks occurred to me. It was as if I were there, somewhere else in time. I was remembering names of people, ports that I had been to, and yes, even people I had killed.

The intensity of my memory started to fade. Buck tugged on his leash and growled, and I felt a hand on my shoulder. It startled me and I turned with a jerk to see a man with a dark trench coat and a walking stick.

"I'm sorry to have startled you. Are you okay?" he asked.

"Yes, I'm fine, just a little disconcerted" I said. "How may I help you?" I asked. "My name is William Breeley," he said, as he reached out to shake my hand. He was staring at me as though he was studying me or as if he might know me. "Are you Matthew Stein?" he asked.

"I am, sir," I answered. "What can I do for you?" "Were you a university professor?" he asked.

"Why yes I was, but it has been some time ago since I was there." I answered. "Why do you ask, and why do you want to know who I am, and where I worked?" I asked.

"You probably wouldn't remember me, even though I took a semester in World History from you there. I was a lot younger then, but I was really into your teachings of the trade and shipping routes during the 1700s." he said.

"Well, I'm happy that somebody enjoyed my class anyway." I replied. "Why are you seeking me now?" I asked.

"I need to discuss a matter of great importance concerning a lost treasure," he said.

"I'm not a treasure hunter," I said, "and I must be on my way home; my dog needs to be fed."

He asked, "Mr. Stein, could you spare ten minutes of your time?" I replied, "No."

"Please sir, five minutes then?" he asked. I quickly answered him, "Not today."

He then asked, "Perhaps some other day?"

I replied, "I think not, I . . ." He then interrupted me and gave me his card. He told me, "You might find our conversation quite . . . fulfilling." I said, "Thank you," and I turned to walk Buck back home.

When I got home, I took Mr. Breeley's card from my overcoat and put it on the end table next to my chair. I then fed Buck and started a fire in the fireplace, poured myself a brandy, and sat down to warm myself.

As I was staring at the fire in the fireplace, things started to appear ships, ports, and people. I heard laughter, shouting, and pistol fire; there was the passing of liquor bottles and jugs. I saw a ship being loaded with cargo and crews moving about its decks.

I stared at its front bow on the starboard side and saw the name *Intrepid*. I saw the captain standing by the keel wheel wearing a British uniform. The flag the *Intrepid* flew is of the first fleet, from the Crown. She has two banks of heavy cannon on the starboard and port sides with a crew of eighty men. Then I saw the first officer, a man in his early twenties. I felt very strange; an eerie feeling came upon me as if I knew this person somehow.

As my daydream faded, I stood up from my chair with drink in hand and I walked to the fireplace and put my glass on the mantel. I turned and looked at Buck and said, "What is wrong with me? I keep having these dreams about the 1700s and sailing the seas. Is this where I belong? Am I going crazy? I know deep down inside I don't belong in this time. I want to know who Iwas."

As I turned my head Mr. Breeley's card caught my eye. I walked over, picked it up and wondered who this man is and what does he want from me. Why is he so persistent in talking with me about lost treasure? Why is this treasure so important?I'm not a treasure hunter. He is a stranger, I don't know him, and should I trust him? I decided to wait awhile before contacting Mr. Breeley. I was more interested in the *Intrepid* and these visions I was having.

Three days later I went to the university's library to look up information about the *Intrepid*. I read about how she sailed to a variety of ports. I also found information as to the role she played as part of the British fleet. The *Intrepid* was a cargo transport vessel. She carried trade goods to and from the Crown's ports including her home port.

Somewhere during one of the voyages the ship was lost at sea. I was less interested in that part of her history. I was more interested in knowing more about her crew, especially the officers. I found some sketchy information about Captain Phipps and his first officer, John Harriman Pierce. The account ended abruptly as if Pierce may have disappeared. I wondered if he had been killed or transferred to another ship. I spent most of the day searching for more on John Pierce. I found a book on English sailing ships of the 1700s and 1800s. There is something in it that will help me. So, I checked it out. It seemed very strange that I couldn't find much on him anywhere. Even stranger was that the ship he was on is also missing. Is there a connection? That nagging feeling that you have forgotten something, but you don't know what continues to plague me about the first officer. I had never heard the name before, so I am not sure why I feel this way.

It was a Tuesday morning when I got up to feed Buck and turned on the news to see if they had a report on finding the sunken ship. There was still nothing. I picked up the book I got at the library and looked at it again—maybe I missed something. I didn't find anything new except on the cover I noticed that there was a website printed there for more information. I thought, of course, why not check the website. I should have thought of that first. There had to be some type of material that would be useful. I started toward the computer when Buck kindly reminded me of his morning walk. I reached for my hat and coat and Buck's leash, and out the door we went.

I decided to take Buck to the park instead of going to the bridge down by the river where we usually walk. While we walked, I was wondering about the officer Pierce and how he just disappeared. I had a hard time believing that a high-ranking first officer of the British fleet just vanishes into thin air. Plus, the ship he was on is also gone. I wondered if Pierce may have been on that ship, but there was no record of the *Intrepid* sinking. Could there be, or is there some kind of a connection? I'll check the Internet when we get home.

I decided to take a rest on a park bench. There was a newspaper lying on the end of the bench. I idly picked it up while Buck chased after a gray squirrel. I suddenly spotted a small article about the sunken ship in the Grenadine Islands. I took the paper with me. I took hold of Buck's leash, and we set out for home.

Arriving at the house, I went straight to the computer and started the search for John Harriman Pierce. I found that he was descended from a

British admiral named George Rooke, who captured Gibraltar in August of 1704. I also found that Pierce had joined the British fleet to continue the family's military tradition. I read further and saw that Pierce had a lust for gold. He had brought back several artifacts from the local natives in South America when they sailed there. Pierce had a good rapport with a lot of the crew, and they trusted him. He was a good officer. Through the search I found asmall footnote the testimony written by an unidentified captured sailor. He had jumped ship at one of its ports of call. I sat back in my chair and stared at that statement. I looked down at Buck and said, "Buck, I know who the captured sailor was; it was Frick!"

I closed the Internet down, but saved that page to absorb what I just read—most of all, who was Frick? How would I know Frick? How could his name just pop into my mind? What is going on? It was getting late, and I was getting weary trying tounderstand all these confusing thoughts. So, I decided to continue in the morning.

I took William's card off the board Wednesday morning and I stared at it and thought very hard about calling him. After pacing the floor for a few minutes trying to make up my mind, I just reached for the phone and started dialing. The voice in the receiver said, "This is William."

"This is Matthew Stein." I replied.

"I thought maybe you would call, but I had expected it to be sooner than this." William said.

I told him, "I needed to feel right about this, and I was wondering if you could meet me at my place today if you had some spare time?"

William said, "I could meet you later this afternoon."

I replied, "That would be fine, and I'll give you my address." Hanging up the phone I thought I'm not too sure what will happen by meeting with him, but I am curious. Why does he feel talking with me would be a fulfilling experience? By listening to him and his questions I can answer the ones that are plaguing me. These strange visions, feelings, and thoughts must be coming from somewhere.

It was later in the afternoon when a knock sounded at my door. I went and opened the door, "Hello, Mr. Breeley," I said.

"Mr. Stein how are you," he asked, as he reached to shake my hand. "I'm doing fine, please come in," I said.

"It's a pleasure being here" he said as he stepped inside. "I hope we can answer each other's questions to help us understand what is going on here," he said.

William was standing there with a broad smile, like he was going to say something, but he just stood there looking around the house. He stands about five foot nine inches with a stocky build and walks with a slight limp on his left side. He is younger than me, close to fifty I presumed. His face is weathered, and his dress was odd, somewhere around the mid-to-late 1940s. His eyes are seawater blue and a little squinted but are quick to see detail around him. He has light red hair with a beard and no mustache. He is a curious man, that is for sure. "This is a nice place you have here Mr. Stein," he said.

"Thank you. It's not too big, it's just right for Buck and me," I replied.

"Let me take your coat and hat and make yourself comfortable in the living room." I spoke. "Would you like a cup of coffee or maybe a drink of some kind?" I asked.

"I'm fine, thank you," he said, taking the chair closest to the fireplace.

"Mr. Breeley," I said, "The reason why I asked you over is . . ." but he interrupted me.

"The both of us have a lot of questions to ask each other, that's for sure, but I would prefer to be addressed by my first name, William, or even Will, if that is okay with you."

I smiled and said, "Of course, William, and you may call me Matthew or Matt." "William," I said, "some weeks ago you wanted to talk to me about a lost treasure, is that true?" I asked.

He said, "Yes, that is true."

"Were you inquiring about the sunken ship the *Shark* they are looking for now?" I asked.

He sat back in his chair and smiled up at me and said, "Yes, but, Matt, it's not just this vessel; there are others that haven't been found yet," he said.

I gave him a puzzled look and asked, "What do you mean by others?"

"I know there are more vessels that were sunk in the area the salvage companies are searching. The *Shark* is the most important because of its cargo. I have a feeling you might know where she's lying," he said. Then he told me, "I think you might be having some unusual daydreams or thoughts that may appear too real to contemplate. Is that true?"

"Well, I think that, uh . . . to be honest with you, I really wasn't going to tell you the truth. I was going to say I don't know what you're talking about. However, this is true, but how did you know?" I asked.

He said to me, "Matt, I am having the same dreams and thoughts as you. I don't know what this is about, but I have been able to salvage and save the cargo from the ships that I have been able to locate. I am returning all of it back to the rightful country of origin. My dreams and thoughts are to find these ships and to make amends with my past and ease my soul's conscience. My visions have taken me in a different direction from yours.

When I was taking world history courses from you years ago, I was having these dreams then. I also noticed that you were very precise and too detailed about certain areas of the mid-Atlantic, to be exact," he said. "Africa, the South American areas, all their ports, islands, and even the weather and the ocean tides were too real to be a part of history. It was as if you were sailing and describing it as if you were actually there." Then he asked me, "That is true, right?"

I told him, "It is true, but . . ." I stopped and looked at him. I was shocked that he knew so much of what I was thinking that I didn't know what to say.

"I was interested in world history when I was in high school. When I went to college it was my major, and I was good at it," I told him.

"I know that, but do you really know why you were so good in world history, and so precise with everything?" he asked me.

"William, I really can't answer that question properly right now. I can tell you this: I think it was because I had a huge interest in the 18th century and how the world did its trading by shipping," I told him. "But the people during that period played a big part of me wanting to know that century and how they lived and survived." I spoke. "William, I want to know if my knowledge of this time frame has to do with what you meant about other ships that were sunk and may be their location." I spoke.

He said, "We both will find the answers to that question later. I'm going to tell you that I have done a lot of research on certain ships in the 18th century, and of their fates—not just the ships, the crews also. I want to find these other ships and return the cargo back to the rightful owners. I have kept all of the textbooks and paperwork from my classes to help me achieve my goals. I have also kept track of you."

"Why me?" I asked.

"Because of your precision in direction of the seas and ports. It was clear to me that you could help me find these other lost ships," he said.

"Do you want the information so you can make yourself rich?" I asked. "I'm not interested in wealth and fame for me or anyone else. If this is all you want, then you can leave and never contact me again," I stated.

He said, "Whoa, calm down, Matt. I'm not a part of that either. I told you I'm not seeking fame or wealth and I don't consider myself a treasure seeker. I'm telling you none of that is my goal or future. I want to find these ships and return their cargo to the rightful owners so I can ease my conscience, that's all."

"I'm sorry for being upset, William, but there are a lot of people out there who would like to take advantage of me if they knew what I know," I replied.

"I have been following you for years, I even have gone to the library to see what books you checked out. I have been watching you take your dog for walks and studying you and wondering how I was going to approach you with all of this. I felt you were wanting to know who you really are. Just like I was wanting to know who I was by looking for certain information from long past. I did this by looking at the books you have checked out. When you checked out the book on English ships from that era, I knew it was the right time to contact you," he said.

"Matt, I would like to ask you if you have been having dreams and thoughts of sailing ships and envisioning yourself on these vessels. You have, haven't you?" he asked.

I answered, "Yes, William. I have. They seem too real; I can see ports, ships, and their crews."

"Matthew, I would like to ask you a couple of questions if you're up to it," William replied.

I told him, "I'm sorry, this is just too much to comprehend at one time. I am very tired, and I need to rest now. Please excuse my rudeness," I said, "but I must ask if we can continue this later."

He said, "My apologies. I am sorry for staying so long; please forgive me. I am afraid my excitement with getting to finally talk with you made me lose track of time.

I went to get his hat and coat as he stood up from his chair.

He asked, "Would it be okay if I come back soon and talk to you again?" I said, "That would be fine, maybe in a couple of days or so." William said, "That will be great. I will look forward to our next meeting. Good night."

William called a few days later and I ignored the phone and didn't return his call.

I felt I needed more time, like two or three more days. I just wasn't ready yet.

On my trip to the grocery store I picked up a newspaper and saw an article about the *Shark*. They had not found the wreck, but what they did find was a pure gold cup that was believed to have been made by the Aztecs. Their search was continuing in that area. I bought the paper and left for home.

When I got there, I found a message pinned to my door. It said, *please call me as soon as you can*, and was signed *William*. I went into the house and put everything away. I fed Buck and called William, but he wasn't there, so I left a message. I then went to the computer to look up Aztec gold. I wanted to know if the gold cup they had found really was Aztec gold. What I found was the Aztec had indeed made cups, jewelry, coins, and other pieces. There were some pictures of artifacts from museums, so I printed them out, to compare them to the one they found, it looked the same.

William called about this time. He asked, "Matthew, how are you doing? Is everything okay?"

"Hello, yes, Will, I am okay; everything is fine." I replied.

"I was wondering if we could continue our talk again?" he asked. I said, "Yes, you can come over this afternoon if you would like."

That afternoon William showed up at my door. "William, come on in," I said.

"Hello, Matt," he said. "You know I was kind of worried that you weren't wanting to see me or talk to me again. I called and you didn't answer or return my call, so I thought you were upset withme."

I said, "Will, I had to digest the information that you told me. It confirmed my suspicions and wasn't I sure how to react to them. So, all in all, it took longer than I thought, and I am sorry aboutthat."

William asked me, "Is it true about you seeing ships and ports in your daydreams from our last conversation?"

I told him, "Yes, all of that is true."

"Matt, have you envisioned anything else, like people and their names or names of ships?" he asked.

"Yes, I have," I told him. "I have seen the name of a ship that reoccurs to me often, and the names of some of its crew."

He asked, "Would the reoccurring ship be the *Shark*?" I answered, "Yes, it is."

He then asked, "But in your dreams do you see any other vessels?"

I told him, "No, not as clearly as the *Shark*. It is the same with the ports not—very clear. I will tell you, though, the people and their names and faces are very familiar to me."

William said, "I'm going to ask you a question and please don't take any offense from it."

I asked him, "What kind of question?"

He said, "It would be about being hypnotized. Have you ever considered that?"

I paused to think about it for a moment, because I had thought of doing this on my own for some time now. William was wanting me to be hypnotized, but why? There was also something else bothering me about our conversation of four or five days ago and I had to ask William about it. "William," I said, "What did you mean when you said you wanted to know who you *were*, instead of who you *are*?"

He said, "I'm sure that if you were to be hypnotized you would find a lot of things out. Not, only yourself but also some of the people who are around you. I think it would help you. You would probably feel much better afterward."

I asked him, "So, would that information include you?"

He said, "Maybe, but you have to find out for yourself, and this is the only way to do that. Are you willing to go through with this or keep wondering who you are?" He asked.

I told him, "I'm not sure if I want to do this, because I may find out some things I don't want to know. On the other hand, it might be the only way it could answer my questions and ease my mind. Before I answer that I need to think about it a little more." I asked him, changing the subject, "Have you read the article in the paper about a discovery they found from the sunken ship?"

He answered, "No, not yet, why do you ask? Does it have to do with the *Shark?*" "No, I don't believe it does," I said. "They found a gold cup thought to be Aztec gold because of its markings."

He then asked, "Do you think it might some of the cargo of the *Shark*, the ship they are looking for?"

I told him, "I think it might be from some other vessel but not the *Shark*."

He asked me, "Do you have a feeling that they might be really close to finding the *Shark?*"

I said, "No, but it could be a different ship that sailed in the same waters as the *Shark*. William, I want to show you something and it must be kept between you and me. No one else must know about this. You may be shocked to see what I am about to show you," I told him.

I went to my bedroom and pulled out a lockbox. I took it to William and asked him, "William, will you agree to keep this just between you and me?"

"I assure you that I will not tell anyone," he said, as he stood up from his chair.

I opened the box. On the inside was a leather pouch with the initials C.R. burned into it. I took the pouch out, opened it, and dumped out four solid gold coins. They were Aztec pirates' gold coins. Each piece had an embossed skull surrounded by some zodiac- style markings near the edge. On the back side there are stairstep-type markings like an outline of an Aztec pyramid. William was astonished. "Aztec pirates' gold coins," he said, as he sat down in his chair abruptly and stared at the coins. Then looking at me, "Matt," he said, in a worried voice, "You aren't going to believe what I'm about to show you." He reached inside his jacket and pulled out a leather pouch which had the initials

S.W. burned into it. He turned it over and four coins fell on the table. They were solid gold with an embossed skull and the same markings on them as mine. I couldn't believe my eyes: two pouches, each with four gold coins from the same century, and both were Aztec pirates' gold. William asked, "Matt, what are the inscriptions on the outer edge for?"

"I'm not sure what the inscriptions are for, but I do know that they are Aztec pirates' gold coins and are from the 1700s." I spoke. "The one thing I couldn't figure out was the initials on the pouches. Were they people or were they something else?" Questions went racing through my mind. William was as shocked as I was.

I asked him, "Where did you find those coins?"

He said, "I got them the same way you did. Don't you remember? Matt, I can't tell you because I feel you wouldn't believe me anyway. The answer to this question and many more would come out under hypnosis. You would then know the truth, but still, you won't believe it. Are you willing to be hypnotized and except the truth or sit and wonder what is happening to you?" he asked. Then he said, "It's up to you."

I said, "I will try to let you know tomorrow if that is okay."

He said, "That is fine but the sooner the better." We both agreed on this point.

Before William left, we agreed to meet here around nine a.m. to discuss how hypnosis works. I had a lot of questions on this matter and I wasn't very thrilled about it. I was still wondering about where he got his coins. I had a strange feeling about this man, but I couldn't put my finger on it. I felt I had known this man for a long while. I also had a complete lack of trust in him.

I went to bed but had a difficult time sleeping. After tossing and turning all night I got up early. I made coffee and watched the news. There was a reporter talking to someone about the gold cup they found. The treasure hunter told the reporter how they were going to search that area heavily. I thought, good luck, you'll need it.

I picked up Buck's leash and took him for a short walk before William showed up. I didn't know what to expect but I certainly had a lot of questions. At precisely nine o'clock a knock came at the door. Opening it I found William standing on the step with a very lovely lady.

"Matt, may I introduce you to Dr. Shirley Walker," William said.

I hoped they didn't notice the shocked look on my face. I wasn't expecting someone to be with William and especially someone as young and attractive as her.

I said, "I am pleased to meet you," as I reached to shake her hand. "Please, won't you come in?" She was a very attractive lady; she stands about five foot five with a slender build. Her silky red hair fell just below her shoulders. Her eyes were a deep jade green. I couldn't begin to guess her age and dared not to. I would guess that she was in her mid to late forties.

"Matt, Dr. Walker is one of the world's top hypnotists and she agreed to come and talk with you," he said. He then turned to her and said, "Matthew is the one I have been telling you about."

I was surprised because I thought William and I were going to discuss this before I agreed to the procedure. I thought he had assumed too much for me.

William said, "Matt, don't get angry. This is why I brought her here, so you can ask her about the procedure and not me. She is the only one who can answer your questions. Matt, Shirley has had me under hypnosis several times and has gathered a lot of information for me. She is here to answer your questions; then you can decide what you may want to do. You know you should talk with her Matt; she can help you," he said.

I paused and thought for a moment. First, I thought that if I said yes, what would I find out about who I really was? Second, would I be able to handle the truth? But I did want to know who I was and whether my soul belongs in another time.

I answered him, "Well, I guess this might be the only way I get the answers I'm looking for. "Let's go into the living room; it will be more comfortable to talk about this procedure there."

I took their coats and draped them over the back of a chair in the hall. I then led the way into the living room. She said, "Mr. Stein . . ."

I interrupted her, "Please, I am very informal about my name; you may call me Matthew or Matt."

She said, "Very well. You can ask me anything about the procedure if you like. I want to know why you are so uncomfortable about being hypnotized."

I told her, "If this works, I may not like who I am and what I may have done to other people. I also want to know why I'm having these thoughts and such vivid dreams about living in a time so long ago. I believe that I was a part of that period in time, and that I have something to do with the destruction of so many lives. I think I might have lived during the 1700s and don't really belong in this time. If that were the case, it explains why I am so uncomfortable about finding out who I really am."

Shirley asked, "Has this been going on for a long time?"

I told her, "I have had this conviction since I was four years old. The dreams of pirates and sailing ships have gone on for as long as I can remember."

Shirley then told me, "Matt, I must tell you that the procedure may or may not work, there are no guarantees. But if it did, we will try to find out who you really are and why you're here. The hypnosis session will be recorded on video and audio, and a doctor will be present just in case."

I asked, "Why do we need a doctor?"

She said, "In most extreme cases, some people can't handle the information that their mind is producing, and the heart rate goes up and they go into coronary arrest.

However, I have never had any patients do that. When we start, each session will only last about fifteen to twenty minutes. We can add time if you think you can go longer."

I asked her, "What kind of questions do you ask?"

She said, "The questions would have to come from you and you only."

I paused for a minute, and then I asked her, "Will there be anyone else besides you and the doctor in the room?"

She told me, "There would not be any other person present unless you requested it before each session."

William asked, "Would it be okay if I could be there?"

I told him, "Maybe later. I need to see how this goes first." Shirley asked, "Do you have any other questions or concerns?"

"Yes, I have one more question." How will I feel when I wake up from each session?" I asked.

She said, "You will be tired and maybe a little nauseated also." The doctor will help you through that and it will get better each session."

William asked, "Well, what do you think? Matt, are you ready to do this?"

"This is something I should do but I need a little time to ponder this situation. If I choose to do this, I will get back to you, Shirley, and let you know," I said.

"We will leave now and let you contemplate your decision," she said, standing up and walking toward the hall and her coat.

The next morning, I had my radio on and a short newsbreak came on about the gold cup they found. It seemed that a museum had been broken into some years ago and the cup they found was a part of the stolen property. It came from the Aztec ruins that some archaeologists had found decades earlier. It wasn't connected with the sunken ship they were looking for at all.

I was mulling over what questions I wanted to ask, such as, who am I really? Do I belong in this time? How did I get here? I also was asking myself about William Breeley, who was he? How did he know so much about me? I wanted to know the answers, but where to start? I know they can't be answered all at once, if they can be answered at all. If I chose to be hypnotized, would it work or not?

I was asking myself these questions over and over again. I had to get out and do something to clear my mind for a while, so I decided to take Buck for a walk. It seemed my dog was my only true friend, and he does help me get my mind off of things.

We left just after lunch and went to the park where Buck likes to run. I seem to relax better when I watch Buck run around chasing squirrels from tree to tree. He was good therapy, but still I had to make a decision about what I was going to do.

Later that afternoon Buck and I were ready to return home. As we were walking, I was wondering about William and asking myself about who he really is. I felt as though we had a close connection sometime in our lives.

It was very late when we finally arrived home. I put Buck's leash and my coat and hat away. The answering machine light was blinking, William had called. He wanted to know if I was ok and if I had made a decision. "Please call," he said. I saved the message and poured myself a drink and decided to call him later. I still needed more time.

It was Thursday morning when I decided to look up the area where they were looking for the *Shark*. They still hadn't found the ship yet and they were searching in the same area. They were looking too far to the West. I had to wonder if I really wanted them to find it or not. I wondered if they did, what would it mean to me or would it mean anything at all.

I knew that I needed to make my decision then about being hypnotized. It was time to go forth and get my questions answered. I went into the other room and looked for the card Shirley had given to me. I sat down in my chair and picked it up off the lamp table. I was very nervous about making this call. My hands were shaking slightly as I dialed the phone.

Hello, Dr. Walker?" I asked. "Yes," she said.

"This is Matthew Stein. I hope I'm not bothering you at this time, but I was wondering if you had some spare time so we could talk."

"Well, let me look at my schedule here," she said. "Yes, I can meet with you in a couple of hours if that fits your schedule."

"That would be superb," I replied. I then told her, "I would like to discuss some things about the hypnotic sessions that may take place."

"Yes," she said. "I think we should talk about what is on your mind and proceed from there."

"That sounds like a good plan." I spoke. We then said our goodbyes and hung up.

Later that afternoon Dr. Walker knocked on my door. Opening it, I invited her in out of the rain.

"I want to thank you for coming over on such short notice." "That's quite all right, Matthew," she replied.

"May I take your coat?" I asked. "Why yes, thank you." she said.

"Please let us go to the living room to talk. I just made a fire. Would you like something to drink, coffee or may be a glass of wine?" I asked.

She said, "A glass of wine would be nice." She then asked, "Have you made a decision on your hypnotism sessions?"

I told her, "I have decided I would agree to try it. If I say I want to quit, will you do so without any questions?"

She replied, "Matt, I never question my clients when they want to stop. They make their own decisions."

I sat back in my chair to think for a second and asked her, "When would we start?"

She replied, "There is some paperwork to be signed and I need a day to get my video and recording equipment ready. I also need to ask the physician I use if he would be available. Then I will call to set up a time to sign the paperwork and schedule your appointments."

"That sounds good," I said, "But I have a request to ask of you. Please do not tell William about my decision to do this. I will tell him myself."

"Matt," she said, "you told me that you wanted me to address you as Matthew or Matt. Well, you may call me Shirley if you like. All information concerning my clients is considered confidential and no information would be released unless it was by a court order or by the client. This is our strict policy between me, my staff, and all of my clients. If you choose to tell anyone, it will come from you alone." She said, "I will contact you in a couple of days to sign the paperwork and give you the time and the day we would start."

"That would be fine." I told her.

"Matt, I need you to have at least three questions for me to start out with. They will lead to more questions as the session's progress. Before I leave, I would like to talk a little bit about why you feel this is necessary," she said.

"Well, I don't think I belong in this time and I feel my soul has moved from one body to another but from a different time. I feel my soul is stuck in this present-day body and I'm truly someone else," I explained.

She asked, "What period of time do you feel you're from? Is it a hundred years ago or maybe even more?"

"I feel I am from the eighteenth century and I need to get back there somehow." I said. "I also want to know who I was and if I was a good or bad person."

As she listened, she took notes in her tablet. Taking a sip of her wine she said, "I think I have enough to get started and I will contact you in a couple of days." Before she left, she reminded me, "Matt, don't forget to write down the three questions to ask. This is an important part of the process."

I helped her into her coat and said, "Goodbye, and I won't forget. I will bring them with me."

William had called the day before. I still wanted to wait before returning his call and letting him know about my decision. I would call him the next day and tell him that I had decided to go through with the sessions. I know he would want to be there, but I would not allow him at that time. I would write down the three questions the next day too.

Buck woke me up wanting to be fed and needing to go for a short walk. We took a fast-paced walk. I needed to concentrate on my questions for Shirley. When we returned, I fed Buck and sat down at the kitchen table with a notepad and pen. I thought for a minute and my first question was, who am I? My second question was, what year is it? Question three was, who is William Breeley?

After I wrote down the three questions, I decided to call William. "William, I have a bit of news for you."

"Yes, Matt, what's the news?" he asked.

"I have decided to undergo hypnotic treatment." I spoke.

"Matt, that's great news," he said. "I was wondering if I could sit in on some of your sessions," he said.

"Will," I said, "I think not at this time. I feel that I would be more comfortable if I could get these first three questions answered for myself without you there. I think maybe later as we progress through each session."

I knew William was disappointed, but I felt that I really wanted to keep the first few sessions private, at least for now.

William replied, "I understand, and I respect your wishes and hope that you will get the answers you are looking for." He then asked, "Would you let me know how everything is going and call me if you need too?"

I said, "Yes, I will keep you updated."

He then said, "Matt, I wish you well and thank you for calling. Talk to you soon."

I felt he was wanting more from me than just to know who I really was, but I couldn't put my finger on it.

Later that morning Shirley called. She said, "I have the papers ready for you to sign." Will you be home later today?"

I said, "Yes, I will be here all day."

"I will be in your area early afternoon and can bring them by then if that is okay with you," she said.

"That works for me," I said. "See you later."

Shortly after lunch Shirley knocked at my door. "Please come in," I said.

She took some papers out of her briefcase and laid them out on the kitchen table. She had the areas highlighted where I was to sign. She told me, "Read it first and if you have any questions about any part, just ask." I read it and had no questions, so I signed the papers.

She told me, "We will begin our first session in a few days. Do you have your three questions ready yet?" she asked.

I told her, "Yes, I my questions are ready." I also told her, "I called William and told him that I decided to go through this treatment."

She asked me, "Did William have a problem with you not letting him be there for the first session?"

I said, "It seemed as though he did not, but I had a strange feeling he wasn't telling me the truth."

She said, "It would be a lot better if you could be alone in the first four or five sessions. I need you to be at ease and relaxed with no one there but me, the doctor, and you." She also said, "I understand, though, why he may want to be there, and why you don't want him there at this time. This is your decision and yours alone."

"Thank you," I said.

She asked me, "Are there any other questions you may have?" I replied, "Not at this time."

"Well then, I will contact you later, as soon as the paperwork is certified and filed," she said.

As Shirley was leaving, she said, "Thank you, I am very much looking forward to working with you, Matt."

"Yes, I feel the same, but I am very nervous about the whole thing." I spoke. She said, "Everything will be okay, Matt," as she walked out the door.

After she left, I lay down to rest and fell asleep and had a dream of a ship battle. One ship was flying a Spanish flag and the other was flying a black flag with skull and crossbones on it. The name *Shark* was painted on the side. The Spanish ship was hard to make out, but I finally saw the bow of the ship. It said *La Flora Cruz*. I saw men being killed by pistol fire at close range. It was so close I could see the powder burns on their skin. Men were being slashed with swords and knives; arms and legs were being cut off along with fingers and ears. The cannons were blasting through the ships' masts and cutting men in half as the cannon balls exploded. I heard the screams of men as swords were thrust into their chest cavities and abdominal area. There were blood and body parts everywhere; it was a ghastly scene. I tried to concentrate on the captain of the *Shark* and noticed he looked like John Pierce, but it couldn't be because I heard a voice call out his name, Captain Rue.

My dream faded and I awoke breathing heavily and perspiring profusely with a big question on my mind: were the *Shark* and the *Intrepid* one and the same? If so, then Captain Rue and John Pierce must be the same person. If this was true, then that was why I couldn't find more information about him. His name had changed.

I thought about this all day and that evening just after my walk with Buck I sat down to watch some TV. I was skimming through the channels and happened to come across a news brief about the sunken vessel. One of the divers had found a part of the bow that had a brass nameplate attached to it. I watched with high hopes but at the same time I felt they weren't going to find the *Shark* in the area where they were looking. I was intensely curious, however, what ship might be lying in the same waters as the *Shark*. It seemed like a long time before the diver came up with the plate but when he did my heart started to race and I leaned forward to get a good look. A man lowered a basket to the diver so he could put the plate in it, but it was still attached to a board from the ship and they wanted to save as much of it as they could. The diver finally got the piece in the basket and it was hauled aboard and put into a washtub of fresh water. This would help preserve the wood. They cleaned the brass plate and held it up to the camera to show its name. It was *La Flora Cruz*.

I couldn't believe that just last night I had a dream about this same ship. I remember reading about these ships and their trading methods. This was a Spanish ship that transported wine, rum, and textiles to South America. Then they traded for coffee, wood, and clothing material. In between their usual ports of call they would make various island stops and trade for gold and silver with the natives. This was probably why this ship was at the bottom of the sea. I sat back in my chair and was relieved that it wasn't the *Shark*.

The next day was uneventful, except for my curiosity. I remembered I asked William, when we first met, about him being a treasure hunter for self-gain. He told me he wasn't looking to make money off of these countries but if they offered a donation toward what he was doing, that was a plus. He said he was looking for these ships for other countries and returning the salvaged cargo to its rightful owner for unpaid services. I wanted to know if William was a part of the company that was looking for the lost ship. I went to the Internet to find out who was doing the search. It was a museum from South America that was funding the search. This answered a question that came to my mind when I first met William. The museum is paying for those services and William is not accepting payment.

Three days had past and I hadn't heard from Shirley, so I thought I might contact her. Just as I was going to do just that, the phone rang. "Hello," I said.

"Hi, Matt." It was William. He asked, "Have you had your first session yet?" I told him, "No, but I think that Shirley might call today."

He said, "I saw on the news that the treasure seekers were on the northwest side of the Grenadine Islands thinking the vessel was there. Have you seen that?" he asked.

I told him, "I haven't had a chance to watch the news yet." I took a big sigh and said, "Thank God," to myself, because I felt they might be getting close.

I didn't tell William that, though. "Will," I said, "Shirley is trying to reach me, so we need to cut this short. Thanks for the phone call. I'll call you later."

I pushed the button to answer Shirley's call. "Hello, Matt, this is Shirley. Everything is set to go; can you be here this afternoon at two o'clock?" she asked.

I said, "Yes, I will see you then."

She said, "I am looking forward to seeing you. Don't forget your three questions." I arrived a little early and checked in. Shirley came out to greet me. "Hi, Matt," she said. "I'm glad you made it. Did you bring your three questions?" she asked. "They are right here in my pocket." I replied.

"Please come with me and I'll take you to your room," she said. We went down a hallway she opened the third door on the right. As we entered, I notice a couch up against the wall closest to the door. Sitting on the couch was a gentleman who appeared to be in his early sixties. His silver hair set off his brown eyes. As he stood, his slender six-foot-five frame and large hands made me think he would have made a great basketball player.

"Mr. Stein, I am pleased to meet you. My name is Dr. Steven Adams. Dr. Walker has told me all about you and your case. Do you have any questions for me?" he asked.

"Yes, I do. Why are you here?" I asked.

"I am here to monitor and record your vital signs and administer medical treatment if needed," he said.

Shirley explained how things were to happen and asked me, "Are you ready to get started?"

I answered, "Yes." She then took my coat and asked me to lie down and relax.

She told me to close my eyes and concentrate on her voice and commands.

I listened to everything she said, and the next thing I knew I was in another world.

It was as if I had changed from one century to another. I couldn't believe how real everything seemed and I can still hear Dr. Walker's voice. She then asked me the first question "Matt, can you hear me?"

"Yes," I told her.

She asked me, "Where are you?"

I told her, "I am on a ship out on the ocean. I'm wearing strange clothing and there are men working everywhere cleaning the decks, moving crates, tying ropes, hollering orders, rolling extra sheets of canvas, and climbing tall masts." I looked around and saw that we are at sea. Huge white canvas sails were tugging the ropes, they were so full of the ocean wind. I heard words like "Aye, Cap," "stow away," "batten down" and "quarterdeck." I am standing near a man wearing a uniform with braiding on his shoulders. His hat is feathered all along its edges. His hands are clasped behind him and he has a hard weathered face. He is staring forward as if looking clear across the ocean into the future. He must be the Captain. Next to him is a young man, the helmsman, navigating the ship with a large compass in front of him. Behind me there is another deck about a foot above the level I am standing on. A man leaning forward against the deck banister is using a megaphone. He is barking out orders to the men on the deck belowand to the men on the masts above. The man next to me would say something to him, and then the other man would yell it out to the deckhands. I was standing next to the captain.

I heard Shirley ask me, "Has anyone mentioned your name yet?"

I said, "No, not yet!" But just as I said that the captain turned and looked at me. "Mr. Pierce have the men close the main deck hatches and secure them," he said gruffly.

I told Shirley he said my name: it's "Mr. Pierce."

She asked me the second question, "What is the year you are in?"

I answered, "I don't know yet."

With a very stern voice the captain again said, "Mr. Pierce, did you hear me? I do not wish to give out orders more than once." I turned toward him, apologized, saluted, and said, "Right away, sir." I scurried down the ladder from the mid deck to the main deck and walked over to the men who were lowering guns and cannon balls to the men below. I asked a man who was standing there looking down in the hole, "Sailor, are you about finished here?"

He turned, saluted me, and said, "Aye sir, just a few more crates, then we be done, sir."

I told him, "Be quick about it. The captain wants the hatch secured." "Aye, sir," he said.

I then asked him, "What year is this?" "Sir?" he questioned.

"Sailor, I will not ask you again. What year is it?" I asked.

"Why, 1715, sir," he replied. I then turned and went back to the mid deck and stood by the captain.

Shirley said, "Matt, it's time to wake up now."

When I woke, I felt a little dizzy, but I am wanting to know more. I told her, "It is the eighteenth century, and the year is 1715."

She said, "You have had enough for the first time. We will continue later."

I felt very tired and disappointed at the same time. I really want to know the name of the ship. Another question came to my mind: who is William Breeley? I was excited, though, to find out what year this took place. I made another appointment with Shirley right away.

When I got home the answering machine light was blinking. I thought it must be William who had called. I was surprised to find it was Shirley, "Matt, just checking to see if you are ok. Please call me to let me know."

I immediately returned her call. "Shirley, this is Matt, I am just fine."

She said, "Good, I was concerned since this was your first session. I will see you again on the twentieth at nine am. Please, call me if you feel anything out of the ordinary. Take care and I will see you in a couple of days."

I sat down in front of the fireplace to think about what had taken place. I really felt I was there on that ship. It was hard for me to wait for the next time.

The next morning William phoned. He asked, "Matt, how did things go yesterday?"

"It went well, and I am excited to go back and learn more," I said.

William replied, "I really understand about you wanting to know more. Do you have any reservations about what you are doing?" he asked.

I said, "I am being cautious, but I feel that this is the right thing to do. I want to learn about who I am.

He asked, "Matt, I was wondering if we could meet and discuss this?"

I said, "I would like to go further to have some other questions answered first; then we can discuss what I have found out up to that point." I knew he was not happy about that response.

He said, "Matt, that sounds like a good plan, which works for me." Then he asked, "Would you call me after a few more sessions?"

I answered, "Yes, I will, but please give me more time." After Will and I said our goodbyes I took Buck out for a walk. I felt better knowing a little about my past; however, it created many more questions. Sometime later that afternoon when Buck and I got home I received a phone call from Shirley. She said, "If you have the time I would like to meet with you before our next session. There are a few things Dr. Adams and I would like to discuss with you."

I asked, "When would you like to talk to me?" "Can you be here in fifteen minutes?" she asked. "I'll see you then," I said.

I went to her office and she and Dr. Adams were waiting. She told me, "Dr. Adams and I feel that we are going to let you go longer under hypnotic sleep. Both he and I feel that you are able to handle a little more time." Since you were in such a deep hypnotic state, we feel you should be put on a monitor."

Dr. Adams said, "This can only happen by your permission, however."

I thought about it for a minute then asked, "Will you wake me if you feel something is going wrong?"

"Of course." He continued, "I am going to put you on a monitor and watch your vital signs. It will track your heart rate, breathing, and blood pressure."

"Dr. Adams, as you know I was very apprehensive about this procedure to begin with. After having one session I would like to get started again right away. So, what I am saying is I agree."

Shirley said, "We will continue tomorrow on the scheduled appointment at nine."

When I got to Shirley's office the following day, I asked her, "I want to start where I left off. Is that a possibility?"

She said, "I will try to help you start where you left off, but that sometimes doesn't work."

We went to the same room I was in the first time. I laid down on the bed and Dr. Adams began placing the sensors on my chest. He kept reminding me to relax. This was difficult due to the reality of the monitors and the anticipation of finding out more about myself.

Shirley came in sat in the chair next to the bed and began to talk to me calmly and quietly. I closed my eyes and concentrated on her soothing voice. As my body began to relax, I could still hear talking to me. I felt, weirdly, as if I were in two different worlds.

Shirley said, "Matt, the year is 1715 and you're on a ship, giving orders to some men to close the hatches on the main deck. The person you are standing by, is he the captain?"

I answered, "Yes."

I had told the men to close the hatches and went back to the mid deck and stood by the captain. The captain told me to go to the lower deck and check on the men there. Saluting him, I said, "Aye, sir," then carried on. When I reached the main deck, I walked across toward the door that went down to the lower deck. I passed the mainmast and looked up to see how big it was, but something shiny caught my eye, a brass plate nailed to the mast. I walked over to look at it and it read *The Intrepid Commissioned in 1709 British Fleet.* I continued toward the lower deck door, walking through a poorly dressed and exhausted-looking group of men. As they saw me coming, they stood and saluted me and said, "By your leave, sir." Some also smiled, showing their rotted or missing teeth.

Everything below was in order, so I went back up topside. All three masts had men in the crow's nest. Looking straight up at the mainmast, I saw a man in the aft mast crow's nest lean over and heard him yell down to the captain, "Land ho!" Everyone scurried to the port side to look, but the captain ordered them back to work.

I heard some of the men say, "It will be good to be home again." I asked one of the men as he approached me, "Sailor, what port are we entering?" He looked at me as if I were daft, but he told me anyway, "Why, sir," he said, "we are in the Bristol Channel heading to Portishead Pier."

We were in Britain, but why I didn't know. I do remember though, in the seventeen hundred the British shipping went from Britain to Africa to South America and back again through the same shipping lanes; this could be a return trip.

I turned to look at the captain, but he was gone. I then asked another officer where the captain's quarters were, and he said they were where they'd always been, with a chuckle. Again, I got the "Are you daft?"

look like the officer answered, "At the stern, sir, one deck down" with a confused expression on his face. I thanked him and asked if this was a return trip. He said, "We were to come home with our cargo and we haven't been home for a year."

I thought I had better be more careful with my questions, as the men were beginning to look at me with suspicion. I began to wander and learn my way around the ship. As I started to walk, things began to take on a more familiar look. I remembered that the farther down into the hull I went, the heavier the smell of mildew and foul odors became. I remember where the crew sleeps, the cargo holds, and the gun deck. I got to the gun deck when a lieutenant approached me and asked if everything lookedshipshape. I said it looked fine and moved forward. I heard someone call my name to come on deck. The captain wanted to see me. I went topside and there he was glaring at me as if I had done something wrong.

"Mr. Pierce," he said, "we will be in port tomorrow morning and you are to dine with me tonight. Be there at six bells sharp; I have something to share with you."

"Aye, Captain," I said. "I'll be there."

Shirley gently talked me through waking up. She said," Matt, it is time. We can continue this tomorrow."

As I woke up slowly, my body was heavy with fatigue and my mouth was dry. I asked, "Is everything okay?"

The doctor said, "Yes, but your blood pressure and heart rate started to rise so Shirley and I agreed it would be best to end here for now."

I left Shirley's office and arrived home, where Buck greeted me at the door. I had forgotten about my poor dog. I thought I better take him for a walk. It felt good to be getting some exercise and fresh air after feeling so fatigued during the morning session. When Buck and I arrived home, there was a message from Shirley's office. My next appointment was for two p.m. tomorrow afternoon. I called back and confirmed it.

The thought of the shipwreck entered my mind and I decided to check the Internet to see if they may have found the sunken vessel. The article said that they had to abandon the search for now because of bad weather. They were not sure when they could resume. I was relieved in one sense but also was sorry in another. I wanted to know if it was the

Shark or not. I was hoping the wreck would contain some artifact that might pertain to me.

Waking up the next morning, I was thinking of why the captain wanted to talk to me. What more did I want to learn from these sessions? I still had no idea what role William played in all of this. I called a dog kennel to see if they could take care of Buck. I didn't want to do this, but I had to, so I could concentrate on my quest.

I arrived at my appointment that afternoon and was greeted by Shirley and Dr. Adams. I was anxious to get started so Dr. Adams immediately attached his monitors and Shirley got me relaxed. I must be getting more at ease with these sessions because soon I was in the captain's quarters.

We were seated at his table. There were two servants dressed in white silk shirts and black pants. One of them was setting a glass of red wine at my right hand, and the other was serving the main course. The captain was sitting at the opposite end of the table. He was staring at me as though he disliked me for some reason.

I asked him, "Are you feeling ill, sir, or have I done something wrong?"

He said very quickly, "I am fine, and you have done nothing wrong, but I have something to say to you." Turning toward the servants he said, "You may leave the room." One of the soldiers entered the room. The captain told him, "Post this door and don't let anyone in."

The soldier saluted and said, "Aye, captain," closing the door behind him.

The captain looked at me and said, "Mr. Pierce, I want to tell you that my trust in the crew is profoundly diminishing."

I asked him, "Sir, why do you feel that way?"

He said, "It's the way the crew looks at me when I pass them by. I have been told that there is a lot of talk throughout the ship. The crew seems to respond to my orders more slowly than they do when you give them orders."

I started to remember that the men would talk to each other about the captain and how he used them to achieve his wealth. He would steal some of the cargo we were transporting and trade it for gold and silver for himself. He told the men he used to keep their mouth shut and he would give them some of the profit, but most generally he never did. If he heard that any of the crew may have said something, he would have them flogged. He never treated them properly, their food was inadequate, and work hours were long, with no sleep. He gave nothing, he shared nothing, except with me. I, on the other hand, did just the opposite, and that is why I think the men respected and liked me. They were losing their trust in him. Some of them were very angry. I remember some of the crew would come to me and tell me they would rather have me as captain of this ship and not Phipps.

The captain continued, "Mr. Pierce, you're my first officer and I know the men have grown to like you. They put their trust in you more than me. You have a lot of friends on this ship and it seems that the crew and most of the officers alike would have you captain rather than me."

"I know you know," he went on, "what we have on this ship and you are to keep your tongue tied about it." He then asked me, "Do you understand?"

I asked him, "Are you talking about the gold and silver below deck?"

He slammed his fist on the table and said, "Mr. Pierce you know damn well what I am talking about. Now do you understand?" I assured him I did.

He told me, "Tomorrow the ship is to be emptied of everything except the one compartment that holds the gold. That I will take care of myself and your share will be taken to your place of residence." He said to me, "You better go and get some rest now and keep quiet about our conversation."

I said, "Yes, sir," saluted and left. Approaching the ladder to the upper deck, a crew member saluted and introduced himself. "Sir," he said, "my name is Skyler Wilkes. If by chance, there is anything I might do for you just let me know."

I really didn't know what he meant but there was something very familiar about this man. I felt I knew him from somewhere.

As I walked around the ship I suddenly knew where my quarters were, just down the hall from the captain's. I saw my name next to the door of my room. When I entered, I saw a mirror on my left, a small desk, and a bunk. I walked over to the mirror and saw myself for the first time. I was not surprised but I take aback a little at my appearance.

My stature was smaller than I expected. My hair was longer; it was pulled back and tied at the nape of my neck. The color was dark brown. I looked like a figure from the book I checked out at the library. Strolling across the room to the bunk, I pulled out a drawer and took out a small, locked chest. Placing it on the bunk, I started looking for the key. I found it hidden between the mattress and the wall. Putting the key into the keyhole, I opened the lid. It was completely full of gold coins. I picked one up and looked at it.

They were Aztec pirates' gold coins. They had the same markings as the coins that I have, with the embossed skull and zodiac-type signs on the front and an outline of the Aztec pyramid on the back. These coins were just like the ones I showed William.

Shirley woke me once more. I said to her, "I feel fine. It seems to have been a short time—is there something wrong?"

She said, "It has been three hours. I felt that was long enough." She told me, "I want to review the tape because I may have heard something important."

Dr. Adams checked my vitals and asked me, "How do you feel?" I said, "I am a little tired but feel I could go longer."

He said, "Dr. Walker and I will discuss your length of time. We will let you know at your next session whether we both agree to let you go longer or stay with the three- hour limit."

I left the examination room and stopped to make my next appointment. The receptionist said, "I can get you in three days from now on the twenty-fifth."

I asked, "Couldn't it be sooner?"

She said, "Sorry, can't do it. Dr. Walker is booked until then. We will see you that day at ten thirty a.m."

I left the office and went home. I was very tired but ate some supper and went to the living room to rest. I took out the gold coins to look at them. As I was staring at them, I was wondering how and why my soul (if at all possible) is in this time period, and why it didn't move on. I asked myself whether we just go to other times from body to body or did I just get stuck somehow in time? What happened to my soul?

A couple of days later William knocked on my door. I greeted him with a handshake and said, "Hello, William, come on in. How are you? Let me take your coat and hat." I asked him, "May I offer you something to drink?

He said, "I'm doing fine and if you have some coffee that would be great." We sat down at the kitchen table as he filled me in on the sunken ship. He said, "Matt, there isn't any change in their search. The reason I came over here is to find out how the sessions are going. How do you feel about what you are learning?"

"William, there are quite a few questions that have been answered but more needs to come about. I know who I am, and I want to know more about me," I said. I told him, "I met a man that was willing to help me if I needed anything." I expressed to William, "I feel I know him, but I can't put my finger on it. William's expression looked like he wanted to make a reply but wasn't sure what to say. So, he said nothing. After a few seconds he asked, "Matt, what about the *Intrepid*? Is it at sea or in a port or where?"

I said, "It is in a British port and will be for a while." It was strange, though; I thought he would ask some other questions but didn't. He said he had to go, and he would be in touch soon.

Three days passed slowly before I went to my next session with Shirley. Shirley asked me, "How are you feeling?"

I said, "I'm feeling fine, but I would like to have longer times during my sessions if that is possible."

She said, "Dr. Adams and I have talked about this and have listened to the recordings. We have looked at your vital records and everything at this point looks normal. We have decided to let you have more time for now and see how you progress."

I said, "Thank you. I'm ready to get started."

I lay down on the bed again and Dr. Adams connected me to the monitors again. Shirley's voice was calm and soothing as usual. I suddenly found myself in my quarters on the *Intrepid*, looking at the gold coins. I heard Shirley asked me, "Matt, is there any other type of gold there?" I looked around and saw a trap door in the corner of my room. I told her, "I see a trapdoor; I will look in there." I went over to open it when someone knocked on my door. I told them to enter. It was Skyler Wilkes. He told me, "My apologies, sir, for the intrusion, but the men want to know if this trip will be a good payoff for them."

I asked him, "What do you mean by that, payoff?"

He said, "The riches that are aboard, the ship seems to be worth a lot."

I told him, "The cargo is the property of the Crown and the crew is being paid to deliver it as such! That includes everything on board this ship."

Skyler looked puzzled and turned to leave but stopped and turned around and asked, "Sir, can myself and a few others come and talk to you?"

I asked him, "About what?"

He said, "About the upcoming plan."

I wasn't sure what he was talking about, but I was curious enough to say, "Aye, go get the men and come back." He then saluted me and scurried off with a smile.

I went to the trapdoor and opened it. There were gold coins along with other gold and silver pieces that filled another small chest. I wasn't sure where it all came from, but I had my suspicions. I closed the door and wondered why some of the crew wanted to meet with me. I felt I had made a promise to them and they wanted me to deliver on it. A knock on my door came just as I sat down. I told them to enter. Several men came in and stood crowded in a line and saluted me. I was nervous because of their demeanor.

They looked as if they had died and returned for vengeance. They had knife scars, missing teeth and fingers, and unshaved faces and they were there to talk to me.

I told them, "I want you to give me your names." They all gave me puzzled looks. Skyler spoke up very quickly and said, "Myself and these mates: Three Finger Qwinn, Dagger Dan, Toothless Tom, and Frick have come to talk about the plan."

Skyler seemed to be the voice of the crew and wanted to be the go-between for me and the crew. I told them, "I want you to just relax and tell me what is on your mind."

They were hesitant and very nervous at first because they were talking to a superior officer. I told them, "Speak up, men; tell me what you want."

Skyler told me, "Sir the men are ready to take the ship and want to do it tonight before we enter the harbor. We are all wondering if this is to happen or not, sir."

I stood up and looked them in the eyes and said, "Men, there is going to be a better time coming up if everyone can wait."

Qwinn asked, "Sir, will the whole crew return because of crews switching ships after each trip?"

I assured him, "If everyone returns and signs on, they will leave with the ship." I also told them, "I want all of you to follow the captain's orders and be patient."

They said, "Aye, sir," and that they would tell the others to do the same. Then they left. I felt I knew what was about to happen, but I was very uneasy about Frick. He was too attentive and not saying anything.

Shirley woke me and asked, "Are you feeling alright?"

I told her, "I am fine. Why did you wake me up again so soon? I thought we were going to go longer."

She said, "I want to have a meeting about this session tomorrow at one p.m." I told her, "I am disappointed, but I will be there."

The next day I went to Shirley's office and went into a conference room to discuss what had happened the day before.

Shirley asked, "Matt, how do you feel about the things that are happening up to this point?"

I said, "I have found out who I am and what year it is. I don't know what to think about the rest, except I feel more at ease knowing that I will find out. I feel I should be there, to bring out the hidden memories of my other past. I feel I'm someone else. I am not trying to stop anything, nor am I trying to change anything. I'm just trying to understand why I am here in another time."

She said, "It seems that things are going to get worse. Are you ready for that?" I asked her, "What do you mean by getting worse?"

She said, "Matt, each time you go under you will discover more about who you were, and you may not like what you find out."

So, I told her, "I need to know who I was, that's all." She told me, "Then we will continue tomorrow."

The next day I went in as soon as the office opened and she told me, "I am going to let you go longer this time." She told me as I was going under, "Your last thought was the night before docking."

After the crew left, I went to my bunk to lay down. At sunrise we lifted anchor and sailed into port; I was topside, and it was good to see land again. All hands were on deck making ready to moor the ship. After the ship was moored, the men opened the guard rail, put the gang plank down, and opened the doors on the side of the ship to unload.

The port was busy; people were milling about—sailors and men looking for work loading and unloading cargo.

The captain gave orders to unload all the cargo and restock the ship with all sailing goods. He said, "When that is done all hands will get paid and have a leave of three weeks. All hands are to return and register to sail again at that time, if they want to sail on the *Intrepid*."

I went down to my quarters and retrieved some of my things. Opening the trapdoor, I retrieved a handful of gold coins and put them in a leather pouch. I left my room and headed topside.

When I got there the Captain stopped me and said, "Your belongings will be taken to your home."

I said, "Thank you, I am grateful; however, I will take care of my own personal things and thank you for being so considerate. I have asked two of the men to help me. We will do this promptly."

At that moment Skyler came to me and asked, "Sir, do you have a coach waiting?"

I replied, "No, I haven't had a chance to call for one yet." He said, "I will, with your permission, locate one for you." "Yes, please do so," I said.

The captain looked at me in anger and said, "I have a crew coming in this evening to empty the cargo holds of the ship at nine o'clock. You are to be here to watch over everything."

I asked him, "What crew is to be here at that hour?"

He said, "The British Guard." He then handed me some keys and said, "These are for the other rooms below. You know which ones I'm talking about. Keep a close eye on them."

"Aye, Captain. I will be here tonight at nine o'clock to unload the rest of the ship." I said.

Skyler approached and said, "The coach is here, and I am ready to help you load your trunks."

I asked him, "Where's your help?"

He said, "I will go get him and meet you outside your quarters."

I took my bags and some of my clothes to the coach, then returned to my quarters where Skyler was waiting. Again, I asked him, "Where's your help?" When he was about to tell me, here came Frick. I turned and looked at Skyler and he said, "Frick volunteered, I didn't think you would mind."

We entered my room and I told them, "Take out the rest of my belongings and I will get everything else ready by the time you get back." When they left, I watched them go topside then I returned to my cabin. I locked the door and went over to get the small chest of gold out of the hidden floor panel. It was very heavy. When they returned, I told them,

"Take the chest to the coach and return to get the big chest by the desk. That one will need two big men to carry it and I will pay them extra." They smiled as if I had done this before. I followed them to the coach, and they put it inside on the floor. I reached in my pocket and gave them each two gold coins. When they saluted me Frick then turned and left very quickly. I stopped Skyler and asked him, "Do you think Frick can be trusted?"

He told me, "I think he could but not too far."

I said to Skyler, "I will see you in three weeks. Oh, also, don't you tell anyone where you got the money."

He said, "I won't, and I'll tell Frick, sir."

As I was standing there, I suddenly realized I wasn't sure where I lived. The driver knew who I was, so I told him to take me home.

The town appeared to be a large military community. There were all sorts of shops and warehouses, and lot of activity. I noticed this as we were leaving town. I asked the driver, "Where are we going?"

He said, "I am taking you to your home as you requested, sir."

I then asked him, "How do you know who I am?" He told me, with a chuckle, "I am one of your servants and I always drive you to wherever you want to go." He told me, "Your home is coming up on your left on the bluff overlooking Portishead Pier." We stopped in front, where a man dressed in servant livery came out to greet me. He opened my door and said, "Welcome home, sir. We are all very happy to see you home again." I stepped out of the coach and grabbed my bag when the servant said, "Sir, I and the others will take care of your things." I told the driver to come back and pick me up before nine p.m. because I had to be back at the ship at that time.

When I entered the house, it was beautifully decorated with an extremely large gold and silver chandelier in the foyer. There was a winding staircase that led to the upper level. It seemed as though there were several rooms upstairs. I asked myself how much I was worth, because the house was opulent. The servant who met me at the door walked up behind me and asked, "Sir, what shall I do with the two chests that were in the coach?"

I told him, "Get some help and take them to my bedroom." I then asked him, "By the way, what is your name?"

With a puzzled look, he said, "Timothy, sir." I asked him, "Timothy what?"

He replied, "Timothy Marks, sir."

I was still standing on the front door landing looking around when Timothy handed me a sealed envelope. He said, "Sir, a courier brought this by earlier today and I am to give it to you upon your arrival." I walked into a seating area with a fireplace and several bookshelves. This must be my library, I thought. I saw what looked like a comfortable chair and sat down. The chimes from a mantle clock sounded seven p.m. I opened the envelope and it said,

I will be there at nine tomorrow morning Can't wait to see you.

All my love, Victoria.

Shirley brought me out of my trance and said, "Matt, it has been a very long time for you to be under, how do you feel?"

I told her, "I feel fine and I am okay, but I need to talk to William."

I left for home and called William, but he wasn't there, so I left a message. I then went down to pick up Buck and he was very happy to see me. I made arrangements to bring him back in a day or so. I left for home but stopped to pick up a paper to find out if the treasure hunters had made any progress. I was relieved to find out they had given up the search for this year because of funding and lack of further evidence of the *Shark* in this area. When I got home, I checked the answering machine, still no message from William.

I decided to take Buck for a walk. I knew by the way he was jumping around he wanted to go too. This was always a good way for me to put some perspective in my life. When we got home, I noticed the light on the message machine was blinking. While I was feeding Buck, I listened to the message. It was Shirley. She wanted me to schedule another morning session in a couple of days. I called her office and asked for my appointment time to be nine a.m. on the third.

Buck's low growl let me know that someone was at my front door. Opening it, I came face to face with William.

"Good," I said, "You got my message."

"Yes," William replied. "That's why I came right over."

I told him, "Please come to the living room and have a seat. Would you like a glass of wine?" I asked.

He said, "No, thanks. I'm fine."

Then I said, "Maybe you might prefer a glass of rum instead."

He stood up very quickly, looked at me and said, "You know who I am, don't you?"

I told him, "I finally put it together and figured it out that you are Skyler Wilkes." He then smiled and said, "It's about time."

I said, "I think this whole thing is about time. William, I'm so confused about all that is happening. None of this is making any sense at all."

He told me, "Matt, calm down. You need to keep going to Shirley—there are more questions and answers to come. When I found out that you and I were connected from past history I too was in shock and disbelief about the whole thing. I also couldn't understand how my soul could just go from one time in history to the next. I feel that it did, and it went with another soul—yours. Matt, I know all the same people on the ship as you do. I also know that your reputation and career is well thought of and I understand the importance of that reputation in the community." He said, "Our friendship will grow in the past and hopefully in the future, but you need to find all of that out on your own. I can't tell you what I found out, because it might change the course of history."

I then asked him, "Do you know if it is possible to change things back then or even now through hypnosis?"

He replied, "I can't answer that. I never wanted to change my life now or then. I just wanted to know who I am. Besides, you should talk to Shirley about that. She is the analyst. Matt, how do you feel about all of this?"

I told him, "Really strange but relieved at the same time." "When are you to go back?" he asked.

"In two days," I said. "Will, I need to ask you how you made the connection with your situation and mine."

He said, "Through the courses I took from you and my sessions from Shirley. With all the information I was getting, it was leading me to you at that point. I then decided to take a chance and approach you, hoping you were the person I was searching for. I wanted to convince you to go see Shirley; that was the only way I would know for sure. Matt, I really have to go, and I will be out of town for a while, but I will leave my phone number with Shirley if you need to talk to me."

Before he went out the door, I said to him, "You are S.W. aren't you, you know, on the coin pouch?"

He smiled and said, "What do you think?" Then he turned and left.

The two days passed, and I went back to Shirley's office after taking Buck back to the kennel. I told her, "I talked to William and told him I know who he is, but I need to know from you if I'm in for any more surprises through these next sessions."

She said, "Matt, I don't know, because your experiences will be different than those of William. I am surprised about the whole thing anyway with William and your connection in two different times. I can't believe he even told you. No matter what, you should continue to learn your side of the story."

I said, "I want to go longer and stay on track. I want to know the whole story." "William/Skyler will be your close friend in either time," she said.

Before she put me under, she said, "You were reading a note from Victoria."

I stood up from my chair and called for Timothy. When he arrived, I asked him, "Would you lay some fresh clothes out for me? I am going to get something to eat."

I went to the kitchen and saw a servant there. I think I may have startled her.

She said, "Hello, sir," as she curtsied "Is there something you may desire Sir?" I said, "I would very much like something to eat."

She said, "Very well, sir, I shall serve you promptly."

I was looking around in the kitchen when she said, "Excuse me, sir, your meal is on the table in the dining room."

I thanked her and proceeded there. I walked into a huge room that had two crystal chandlers, a large dining table, and two fireplaces, one at each end of the room. I turned and looked at the table and saw a large, cooked chicken with potatoes and vegetables, too much for me. I took what I wanted and ate my fill.

Timothy came and told me, "Sir your things are laid out and waiting for you." I asked him, "Timothy, have you eaten yet tonight?

He said, "No, sir."

I then asked him, "Have any of the servants eaten yet?"

His answer was still "No, sir." Then he explained, "Sir, the help does not eat until the Lord of the house does so first."

I told him, "Timothy, please go tell the others to come and eat what's left on the table."

His shocked reply was, "Oh no, sir, we dare not, because of our status. We are here to serve you."

I walked up to him and looked him in the eye and said, "Even though I pay you to serve me, you shall do what I ask of you, right?"

He answered, "Yes, sir."

Then I told him, "Please go tell the others to come and sit and eat the rest of this food. Oh, by the way, that is an order." I also asked him, "Could you please make a fire in each of the lower-level fireplaces? It is very cold and damp in the house, and you can do that after you have eaten."

I went upstairs and looked for my room. Opening the gold -handled door, I walked into a lavishly decorated room. Everything was gold. The wall sconces, the mantle had gold inlay around the edges, and gold medallions decorated the side panels. There was a gold-framed portrait on the wall to the left of the entry. It was of a very beautiful woman. I knew her; it was Lady Victoria Ann Rothader. Victoria came from a very wealthy titled family in Britain. Her father was a huge landowner and a member of Parliament.

Timothy announced, "Sir, the coach is waiting."

I was changing clothes and told him, "I will be right down."

As I was crossing the room, I saw my two chests of gold. Opening the smaller, I took out a few coins for the coachman. That is when I noticed another chest. It was slightly larger than mine and I had never seen it before. I went over to see if it was

locked; it wasn't. I opened it and it was full of gold coins. This must be my share that the captain was referring to. I will deal with this later, I thought. I hurried downstairs and Timothy was standing there with my hat and coat.

He said, "Sir I will be here to greet you when you come home." He also told me, "Sir, myself and the rest of the servants would like to thank you for the extra food and your thoughtfulness."

I said, "Timothy, you are quite welcome and there are going to be changes made that will be for the better. Could you please take care of the chests in my room and put them in my closet?"

He said, "Yes, sir, I will take care of it right away."

I climbed into the coach and the coachmen drove me to the pier. When we arrived, there were several coaches built for heavy loads of cargo.

They were accompanied with a squad of military personnel, including the drivers.

A sergeant came to me and said, "The men are ready to get the special cargo off the ship sir."

I told him, "Follow me, sergeant." I looked about to see guards everywhere, even on rooftops, as if they were expecting trouble. I went aboard and had the sergeant follow me down to the deepest part of the ship. There were eight locked doors about midship, four on each side. He then asked, "Sir, may I have the keys?"

We opened the first door and there were sacks of silver. I took a lamp and held it over one of the opened bags. I couldn't believe how shiny it looked even with this type of lighting. It was amazing! I turned to open another door across the hall. This one contained items of gold. There were plates, cups, goblets, candlesticks, coins in bags, small gold bars, and jewelry. I thought, where did this come from? No wonder the crew wanted to take the ship over. The eight compartments were the same, full of gold and silver worth millions. I told the sergeant, "I am going topside and you are in charge, so carry on."

"Yes, sir," he replied.

I went and stood near the catwalk and watched as the men were loading the coaches when a man in a cloak walked by me and glanced my way. I wasn't sure but it may have been Frick. I wondered why he would be there. I watched him as he left the ship and scurried off into the dark.

About an hour went by and the sergeant said, "We are finished, sir." I asked him, "Did you lock the doors and close off that area?"

He said, "Yes, sir, the doors are locked, and the area is secured." He saluted and handed the keys to me. I watched them leave but noticed that there were two men at the bottom of the catwalk. I went down and asked them, "Why are you here?"

They said, "We were ordered to guard the ship and when you leave, no one is to go aboard including you, sir."

I walked to my coach and had the driver take me home. Timothy was waiting at the door and took my hat and coat.

I told him, "Timothy you should go to bed because it is late."

"Sir," he said, "don't forget you have a visitor coming at nine in the morning." "Thank you, Timothy. Please have someone wake me in time to dress."

I went into the den and sat down and wondered why no one was to go aboard the ship. I also was wondering why Victoria was coming here so early. What was on her mind? And what had I said to her? The night had passed quickly, and I was already up and dressed by the time Timothy came to my room.

I told him, "Timothy please go and get all the servants together downstairs. I want to talk to them." After he left, I went to the small chest and proceeded to put a handful of gold coins into the pouches that I found in my desk drawer. I took them downstairs with me. There stood ten servants wondering what was to happen to them. I approached each one and handed each a pouch of gold and thanked them for their service. They looked at me as if I were letting them go. Timothy asked me, "Sir are you dismissing us from our work?"

I told him, "No, I just want to give all of you something for your hard work and tell you how much I appreciate all of you." They all thanked me profusely. I then told them to get ready for Victoria and that she would be arriving soon.

Just then I heard Victoria's coach coming up the entry to my home. I stepped out in front along with my servant to greet her. Her coachman jumped down and opened the door, and out stepped an attractive lady. She was petite, a little over five feet tall. She was wearing a sky-blue dress and cloak. The fullness of the skirt accentuated her tiny waist, and the sky-blue lace trim matched the color of her eyes; she was very beautiful. She rushed to greet me and threw her arms around me and gave me a hug. I wasn't sure how to take all of this, so I just stood there. She said, "I am so happy to see you. Is something wrong? You didn't return my embrace." Then, taking my arm, she led me inside. I looked at her with a puzzled look and said, "I feel the same." I wasn't really sure how I felt. She obviously wanted to talk.

I said, "Let us sit in the library; it is warmer and quieter in there. I will have Timothy bring us something to eat."

She said with a giggle, "Nothing to eat for me but I would like some tea."

I rang for Timothy to serve tea. Sitting opposite her, I asked, "How was your trip in from the country?"

She said, "It was long as usual, but I have been here a fortnight waiting for you. I came to the city early to spend some time with Aunt Charlotte and Uncle Harry. I am so glad you have finally arrived, and I am glad to be here with you."

I then asked her, "Why did you come?" She looked at me as if I was astranger and said, "I wanted to see you and to talk about our futureplans."

I asked her, "What plans?"

She said, "John, I am surprised that you would even ask that, because the marriage proposal was your idea. John, are you having second thoughts?" Her voice had a slight quiver, and I thought I saw tears welling up in her eyes.

I told her hesitantly, "The marriage is going to have to wait because I have to leave again soon, but this is going to be my last trip."

She looked shocked and hurt and then said, "Well, then the marriage may not take place at all if that is what your plans are."

I told her, "You know that the navy has always been the way for me. If you can wait until my return, we can be married then."

She said, "I am hurt and disappointed, but I will wait this one last time. I know that it will be another year until your return; I will not wait any longer." This time the tears were definitely there.

I told her, "This I promise to you: it is to be my last trip anyway." She then said, "I would like to freshen-up."

"By all means," I replied. "Timothy, please show her to the guest room."

She was gone for a few minutes, and when she came back, she was more composed.

"May we take a walk in the garden and talk some more? I have missed you. Have you missed me?" she asked.

I told her, "I did miss you and it is so nice to see you again." We really didn't talk about too much of anything, just little things the weather, her brother, mutual friends that had recently said their marriage vows. The day went by fast; we had dinner and talked some more and then she said, "I am leaving in the morning."

I told her, "I am sorry to see you leave, but we will be together soon."

After dinner I called for a coach and escorted her to the door. She gave me a hug and kissed me.

She said, "Send me a post when you can." She hugged me again and kissed my cheek and then said, "I will see you in one year. Take care of yourself." I helped her into the coach, and she waved goodbye. I knew as the coach pulled away; I would never see her again.

Shirley woke me and said, "Matt, it is time for you to wake up. You should go home and relax for the rest of the day." Taking my time, I sat up thinking about the things that were happening. Was I really that cold to women, especially to the one I loved—or did I really love her?

I remembered that I had read about Pierce being a serious and cold-hearted person, but I'm not that way now. I guess that things do change over time. Deep down I really did care for her but had a greater love for the open sea and the adventure of it all. That's why I never married.

Shirley asked, "Matt, do you remember ever having thoughts of Victoria in any of your dreams?"

"I really don't recall her," I replied.

She said, "Matt, I can't stress enough the importance of you going home and resting. I am afraid this is getting to be too strenuous for your body to handle without rest."

When I got home, I sat down and thought about a lot of things, but most of all, would this be my last trip? I guess we will see.

The next day I went to Shirley's office and sat down to talk to her. The first thing she asked was, "How do you feel?"

I told her, "I am well rested and ready to start again."

She said to me, "I listened to the recordings and watched the videos." Then she asked, "Matt, have you kept any records or diaries about your dreams at home?"

I said, "Yes, I have."

"Could you go and get them for me now?" she asked. "I need all of them except for the most current ones. I tried to call you, but you had already left. I truly apologize for any inconvenience."

I wondered why she wanted my diaries. I went home to get them and when I returned, I said, "Could you please keep them safe and not to show them to anyone else?"

She said, "Of course I will keep them safe. They are part of your records and the privacy act prevents me from releasing or sharing them.

"Are you ready to start again?" she asked me.

"I am." I said each time I go under it gets quicker and easier.

I had jumped ahead in time a little, for I was loading the coach up with my chests.

I gathered all the servants together and told them, "I want to tell all of you how much I enjoy your company and what a wonderful job you do here. Thank you."

I told Timothy, "If anything should happen to me, the two chests that are in my closet are to be divided among all the servants. There is a note inside the smallest chest that tells you what to do, and it is sealed by my ring. It is a document that leaves the house, grounds, and possessions to Lady Victoria. I have also asked her to keep the same staff if everyone agrees to stay. I then handed him the keys to the chests. I shook his hand and thanked him as I left.

Timothy said, "Thank you, sir. I will see to your wishes."

When I got to the pier the ship was being loaded with all the last-minute cargo of fresh food and water. The crew was there too, signing on as they were told to do. I saw Skyler and most of the same men going aboard. The captain was standing by the keel wheel watching everyone aboard doing their job. He called to me, "Mr. Pierce get your personals in order and stowed, then come see me."

I saluted him and said, "Aye, captain." When I went below to my quarters there were men cleaning the cannons and putting cannonballs and powder away. The rifles and ammunition were stored in cabinets. As I walked to my quarters, I saw a few men putting swords and knives in a separate room. They all stood and saluted me as I passed by. I saw Frick working in the armory and I stopped and asked him, "You there, is everything put away and locked up?"

He stood up and saluted me and said, "Aye, sir, everything is secured." I then asked him, "Is your name Frick?"

"Aye, sir, it is," he said.

I told him, "I want you to go topside and report to the captain for your next duties." I didn't trust him down here.

I stowed my personals and started up top when I saw the door that led down to the hull where the eight other rooms were; it was locked. I then remembered I still had the keys to those doors, and they were in my quarters. I turned to go topside when Skyler stopped and saluted me. As he did so he asked, "May I shake your hand, sir?"

I said, "Yes, you may."

He told me, "It is good to be back on board and I hope you are rested and ready for sea."

I told him, "I am anxious to be at sea again, but I am somewhat unsure what may lie ahead.

He told me, "Sir, all of the men came back and said they are ready to sail." I told him, "I will talk to you later. I have to report to the captain now."

When I got on the main deck, I saw crew members still coming aboard. There was a lot of activity. Some were cleaning; others were maintaining the ropes and lines for the sails. The captain motioned me to him; I saluted him as I approached. He asked, "Are you and the crew ready to sail?"

I told him, "Sir, almost."

He told me, "I want you to meet me in my quarters this evening after your watch." I told him, "Captain, I will be there."

He said, "I will then give you our sailing orders and destination. Right now, I need you to carry on and get this ship ready to sail this evening. I want to leave port with the tide."

I finished my duties and then realized I needed to head to the captain's quarters. I knocked on his door, and he told me to enter. I saluted him and approached his desk.

Phipps said, "Please take a seat. I will show you where we are to sail." He then slid a leather folder across the desk towards me. It was tied in the middle with a leather strap. He said, "Go ahead and open it. These are our sailing orders."

I untied it and removed the nautical charts that had the shipping routes we were to follow. The cargo manifests were also enclosed. These told us what we are to pick up or deliver at these stops. I saw that we are to sail to the Canary Islands off the coast of West Africa. The island was Gran Canaria, and the port was Las Palmas. We were to leave some cargo there and pick up some ivory to take to Georgetown, South America.

At this point the captain said, "When we get to Georgetown, we are to trade the ivory for gold bars. The gold is painted gray to disguise it. You are to check each one by scratching the paint to make sure it is gold. You are to do this alone the day we dock. Ten bars of gold will be put in my quarters and you will receive five. The rest will be put in the eight compartments of the ship. We will also be picking up some lead bars to make musket shot and cannonballs. The lead will go aft in the regular cargo area."

I was looking at the map and said to the captain, "It looks as though we sail back to Britain straight out of port from Georgetown. I also see another sailing line drawn on the map that is different from the others. It goes to the Port of Castries in St. Lucia."

I thought for a moment: that is the same place where they are looking for the sunken ship, the *Shark*. It was all starting to fall together now; I knew what was going to happen.

The captain said, "Yes, we will divert there to take on fresh food and water for the long trip across the sea. When we are in port at Georgetown, I will be going ashore for a while. If you have any shore activities planned, you can do them the next day."

I asked him, "How long are we to be in port at Georgetown?"

He said, "Two days only. Now I want you to go topside and tell the men to prepare to make sail. I will be there shortly." I saluted and left his quarters. Skyler met me just before I reached the ladder.

He said, "Sir, the men are growing restless and are ready for your command."

I told him, "Go tell the others to be patient but they must wait for my signal. This is the voyage we will take over the ship."

Skyler smiled and said, "The men are with you." He then turned and left. I was about to go up the stairs when Frick stepped out of the shadows and said nothing. He looked at me as he was heading up topside. What was he up to? I wondered how much of our conversation if any he heard.

I went topside and ordered everyone to prepare the sails.

The helmsman said, "Sir, I am ready for directions and waiting for your orders." The captain came topside, walked to the top deck, and asked me, "Mr. Pierce, are you ready to shove off?"

I said, "Aye, sir."

"Then do so," he said.

I ordered, "Cast off all lines, set the foresail, and get us out of the harbor." We were sailing out of Portishead Pier and into the Bristol Channel when the captain said, "Helmsman, I want you set a course due south. When we reach open water go full sail. I want to make good time."

It was dark as we reached open water. We were finally at sea. I turned to look back and I could see the light of the lanterns glowing faintly on shore, then slowly fading out of sight.

He looked at our heading and said to the helmsman, "I want you to continue this course until morning."

He then said, "Mr. Pierce, I'm going to my quarters and I want you to stand watch for this night." He then left the deck.

I looked up at the clear and starry sky. The night was warm, and the sails were full, and we were making good time. The first night went without any trouble. It always amazes me to watch the sunrise on the ocean. When it was time for the changing of the watch, the captain came topside with the relief crew.

He said, "Mr. Pierce, take your crew below and get some food and rest." As I saluted, I said, "Aye, sir, the night went well."

He said, "I want to meet with you when you are rested." I then saluted him and headed for my quarters. Skyler was waiting for me below when I got there.

He asked, "May I speak to you, sir, before you go to your bunk?" We entered my quarters and shut the door.

I asked him, "Skyler, what is it you want?"

He said, "Well, sir, myself and the crew want to know if you have a plan."

I told him, "I do. Tell the others that it will happen after we leave port out of the Canary Islands. I want to make it clear to you that the crew needs to be patient and I will let you know when the time comes. Then you can prepare them at that time."

He said, "I will let the others know." As he left, I noticed just before he closed the door there was someone standing in the shadows of the hallway. I closed the door and peeked through the space between the door and the frame. I could see the person walk by; it was Frick. He looked at my door and then followed Skyler. I didn't trust Frick; we needed to keep a close watch on him.

As I went to lie down on my bunk, I could hear Shirley's voice telling me to wake up. I sat up on the edge of the bed and she asked me, "Are you okay?"

I told her, "Yes, but I felt I was being more and more drawn to this other time.

How long has it been?"

She said, "About four hours."

I said, "It feels like it's been days and I am feeling that I'm being pulled more and more into that time."

She said, "The longer you're under, the more you will feel that way. Matt, you will be making the same choices and decisions. Your history is being repeated. No matter what you do or say, it will happen that way in that time. These are but shadows of the past."

"But are they? Can I change the course of history by doing something different? Or are those shadows waiting for me to make things right and to finish something? I feel I belong there more than I do here in this time. I don't want to return to this time. My past is where I belong. Is it possible for a soul to return to its own time and fulfill its destiny?" I asked.

She said, "I don't know. I'm not sure what would happen to a person physically here because no one has ever done that. Matt, are you thinking of trying to do that?"

I said, "Right now I am not sure of anything."

She told me, "Matt, I need you to go home and get some rest. We will continue this day after tomorrow."

When I got home, I was very tired and went straight to bed. Exhausted as I was, I didn't sleep well. Some breakfast would help. After I ate, I decided to visit Buck. That would help bring some normalcy back to my life.

He was as excited to see me as I was to see him. I put on his leash and started toward the nearby park for a run. It suddenly occurred to me what would become of Buck if anything should happen to me. I wanted him to go someplace where he would have the same kind of care that he is used to. I need to take care of this and soon. After a while at the park, I took him back to the kennel.

When I reached the house, I thought I should call William. When he didn't answer I remembered he had told me he would be out of town for a few days. If I needed to get in touch with him, I should call Shirley's office. Several minutes later and after all that I still had to leave him a message.

Something Shirley mentioned crossed my mind: soul transference. Who would have information on that subject? I called Shirley's office. "Hello, this is Matthew Stein again," I said. "Is Dr. Walker available? I would like to speak to her."

The receptionist said, "Please hold, I will transfer you."

"Hello, Matt," she said. "Is there anything wrong?"

I said, "No, everything is fine. I just wanted to know if you might have more information on souls moving from one period in time to another."

Shirley said, "I personally don't have much experience in that field, though I do know of someone who could possibly be of some help to you. His name is Dr. Randall Beckley, an M.D. with a degree in psychology. He has a great interest in soul transferences. Also, I must inform you that all of his answers will be based on theory. Because there is no proof that any souls move from one time to another. However, there are people who firmly believe this is very possible."

I said, "He may not be able to answer my questions, but I have to try."

She gave me his phone number and wished me luck and told me we would resume the next day at ten a.m.

I called Dr. Beckley and introduced myself. "Hello, doctor. My name is Matthew Stein. I would like to talk to you about soul transference sometime soon."

He said, "Well, now, Mr. Stein, this sounds interesting. I can meet with you this afternoon at two p.m. if that fits your schedule."

I said, "That will work just fine. I will see you then."

I made myself a cup of coffee and sat down to watch the news. The phone rang; it was William. I asked him, "How are you doing?"

He said, "I have located a sunken ship in the Caribbean Sea." I asked him, "Is it the *Shark?*"

He said, "No, it's not. It only has a few artifacts and nothing too important on it. It's a French ship and we had to call their government to claim it." He asked, "How are things going with your sessions?"

I said, "They are going very well but stressful. William, are you coming back any time soon? I need to talk to you about something of importance."

He said, "I am coming back tomorrow. I will be able to see you then."

"I have a session tomorrow morning, but I can meet with you later in the day," I said.

He said, "That will be fine you can call me when you're ready."

I arrived right on time to meet with Dr. Beckley. His receptionist greeted me and told me she would let the doctor know I had arrived. She then escorted me to his office. He was a tall African American man with a mustache, a receding hair line, and a soft voice. As we shook hands, he asked me to sit down. He said, "I am not sure how I can help. You intrigue me. Mr. Stein. Tell me, what is your interest in soul transference?" At that point I tried to tell him about my experiences I was having with Dr. Walker.

He asked me, "Do you think that Dr. Walker is helping you?" I said, "Yes, because she is analyzing everything that I say."

He then said, "I will tell you that she is the best hypnotist around. She should be able to help you in many ways." He then asked me, "If she is helping you, why are you here?"

"I have other questions that she is not able to answer. That is why I am here. She told me to see you. She also said you may not be able to answer them either," I replied.

"What is it you want to know?" he asked.

"I feel my soul is from another time, that I don't belong in this time period. With that said I'm wondering if it is possible to go back to the time where I feel my soul belongs. Also, I am wondering if it is possible to stay there through hypnotism."

He then asked me, "Are you having thoughts of wanting to stay where you feel your soul should be?"

I said, "Yes."

"Are you sure this is where you want to be?" he asked. I said, "Yes."

He then said, "I think only in theory that it is possible for such things to happen, but with extreme consequences. My thoughts on all time travel be it by machine or by other means such as by being hypnotized is theory. This is because no one has ever come back to tell us if it worked. You should give this matter great consideration before making a permanent decision. Once you have made that decision to remain in the past, there is no guarantee that the person in present time will continue to live.

He said, "Well, then, if you are determined to go ahead and pursue this, I wish you the best luck. Do you have any other questions?"

I said, "No."

"Please keep in contact with me and, Matthew, would it be okay if I could talk to Dr. Walker?" he said.

I said, "I will keep you informed, and it is okay to talk to Shirley." I left his office and went home.

I gathered my important papers. I needed to make out a last will and testament. I must decide how to disperse my personal belongings, the house. and the dog. I sat down and wrote two letters, one to William and one to Shirley.

When I arrived at Shirley's office, I was ready to begin. Shirley asked me, "How did your meeting go with Dr. Beckley?"

I told her, "He has given me some insight on the questions I asked. He also would like to talk to you. I am supposed to keep in contact with him."

She said, "I will contact him and brief him on this case if you give me permission to do so."

I said, "If you think he could help, that would be fine with me. I want to talk to you and William at the same time after this next session."

Shirley put me under. When I woke, I was aboard the ship. I went topside and looked around the main deck. The crew was busy with their duties. The captain saw me and motioned me to come to him. He said, "I want to see you in my quarters." I followed him down to his cabin.

When the door was closed, he turned to me and said, "Mr. Pierce, when we get to the Canary Islands we are to put into port at Las Palmas."

"Yes, sir, I already know about the ivory pick up and cargo exchange." I said.

He said, "Yes, but I am going ashore to get some personal things. I am leaving you in charge. The cargo that will come aboard besides the ivory is thirty barrels of wine, twenty barrels of rum, fifty barrels of salt pork, sixty barrels of hardtack, and fortybarrels of beans. We are to leave some fifteen kegs of powder and ten cases of rifles. Here is the manifest for you to make sure you have the right count. I will be back before your taskis completed. We sail with the morning tide. I don't want to stay in the harbor to long." He turned and walked to a small table and poured himself a cup of tea. "When we leave port, I want to run a skeleton crew at night if the weather holds. Do you have any questions?"

"No, sir, I will take care of everything." I said, saluting, and left his quarters.

Frick was just down the hall. I walked up to him and asked, "Why are you here and not on the main deck?"

He said, "The captain ordered me to swab the lower deck and to secure all cargo." When I turned to leave, the captain opened his door and ordered Frick to his quarters. I thought that was odd and went topside. I called, "Skyler, gather the crew; we have orders."

He said, "Aye, sir." He called out, "All hands-on deck."

They all stood in a group as I told them, "We will arrive in Las Palmas early in the morning. As soon as the cargo has been switched over, we will sail at once."

Someone called, "What about shore leave?"

I said, "The captain is the only one who will be leaving the ship. Now carry on." Quietly I said, "Skyler, I want to talk to you this evening in my quarters and bring Qwinn with you. You are not to say anything to Frick or anyone else."

That evening after supper a knock came at my door. It was Skyler and Qwinn. "Qwinn," I said, "I want you to stand guard at the door and don't let anyone including any of the crew come in. If the captain comes by give two knocks on the door."

He saluted and said, "Aye, sir."

I asked Skyler, "Do you think Frick is some kind of spy for the captain?" He said, "I don't think so. Why do you ask?"

I told him what had happened earlier today, and it looked very suspicious to me. He said, "I can go get Frick and make him talk."

I said, "No, because the captain will have us all flogged. We will let Frick be and just watch for a while to see what happens. The captain is to leave the ship after we dock tomorrow. I want you and Qwinn to follow him but stay out of sight. Don't let the captain spot you. I want the both of you to report back to me as soon as you find where he is going. You are not to tell a soul about any of this. Here are two gold coins, one for you and one for Qwinn." When they left and I went to bed.

The next morning, I got up, dressed, and went topside. I heard that land was spotted. It must be the Island of Gran Canaria. We will put into port at the north end of the island in Las Palmas. I went up to the keel wheel, where the helmsman and the captain were standing. The captain told me, "We should be in port about eight bells. Mr. Pierce, are you and the crew ready to unload the ship?

"Sir, I will tell the crew to get the ship ready to dock and make ready to receive supplies," I said.

He said, "I am taking two men to go with me when I leave the ship." I asked him, "Sir, would you like me to choose the men for you?" He said, "No, I have already done that."

"With your permission, sir, I will get the crew together and make way for the supplies." I said.

He said, "That is best to do that now."

I said to Skyler, "Meet me below deck in my quarters. I will have you tell the others what their jobs are." We went below and I gave him the captain's orders. I then told him, "When the captain leaves you and Qwinn will leave too. Just don't be seen or get caught."

Just before we entered the port, I ordered all hands to drop main sails and make ready to enter the harbor. As we made our way across the reef and into the channel there were two British warships getting ready to sail out of port. I wondered where they were sailing to. I asked the captain and he said, "I think they are headed to the Caribbean Sea."

I asked him, "Are we to join them?"

He said, "No, we are to take the supplies we have for the fleet to Georgetown.

As we docked the ship, the ropes and sails were made secure. The men were scurrying around like ants to get the ship tied down and ready to unload. The second deck down had four ramps that were just above dock level. This is where they unloaded the powder and rifles. We would also receive the salt pork, hardtack, and beans on the same level. The barrels of wine and rum were too be lowered into the cargo hold with theboom in a net made of rope. I was standing by the helmsman when the captain and two crewmen started down the gangplank. He then looked up at me and I saluted. When he reached the dock, he entered a coach. At that moment I saw Skyler and Qwinn right behind him in their owncoach.

I told the crew, "Snap to, I want you to get everything unloaded and loaded before the captain gets back. If you do this, each one of you will earn an extra shilling." They all cheered "Huzzah!" Four bells sounded when one of the men approached me and said,

"Sir, the ship is near loaded. The cargo is being secured; we're near done."

I told him, "When that is done tell the men to eat and get some rest. I will see them before lights out."

I wondered how Skyler and Qwinn were doing and where the captain was. About an hour had gone by when Skyler and Qwinn came aboard.

I asked them, "Where is the captain?"

They told me, "He is close behind us and he has some chests to bring aboard." I told them both, "You two go below get some food. We will talk later."

The captain drove up to the ship; he got out and ordered the men he had with him to put the two small chests in his quarters.

Watching these actions, I had a very strong sense that I was reliving my past. I really felt that I had been here before. I wanted to change things, but I didn't know how. I guess you can't change the past. I wondered if I would have to relive it all to go forward. I wanted to ask the captain about the jewels and the gold in the chests. I just couldn't, even though I knew that is what was brought aboard.

The captain came aboard and asked, "Mr. Pierce, are we ready to set sail?" "Yes, sir, your orders have been completed; the watch has changed, and themen are below," I said.

The captain said, "Be prepared to sail at first light after we take on fresh water." That evening just before dinner I went down to the lower deck to talk to the men.

I said, "Men, I want you to know how well you have done today with the cargo. I am a man of my word." Handing Toothless Tom, a bag of shillings I said, "There is one for each man here." I trusted him to hand them out. They all thanked me as they saluted. As I went out the door, I heard a loud "Huzzah!" I picked up a plate of food and took it to my cabin. I was eating it when a knock was at my door and I told them, "Enter." It was Skyler and Qwinn. "Come in and pour yourself a rum." I said.

"Aye, and thank ye, sir," they said in one voice as they raised their mugs. "Where did the captain go on his travels?" I asked. I already knew, because things were coming back to me in vivid flashbacks.

Qwinn told me, "The scurvy swine went to a house out on the point and met with four men. They looked like they might be Spanish, but we aren't sure. He was there for a long while. When he came out, he had with him two small chests and put them in the coach. He shook hands with them and then he left."

Skyler said, "Myself and Qwinn here followed 'em back to town and he met two officers from the fleet. He gave them each a pouch of something."

I said, "He must be dealing in the jewels and gold for himself." Skyler agreed, "Aye, me and Qwinn thinks the same."

I thought to myself, it must be some kind of black market.

I asked them, "Did he go anywhere else or see anyone else?"

They both looked at me and then at each other. Qwinn said, "Aye, he did meet with someone else."

I asked, "Who?"

Skyler said, "You're not going to like to hear what we are about to tell you." I told them, "You better tell me anyway and make it quick."

They said, "Sir, it was Frick who met with the captain." Several thoughts bombarded my mind at the same time. Why was the captain talking to him? Come to think about it I hadn't seen Frick all day and he wasn't on the ship. This must be where he jumped ship, but why?

I told them, "You need rest. Go get some sleep. I will see you in the morning." After they left, I continued to wonder about the connection between the captain and Frick. During my hypnosis it seemed I could remember things I had read from present time and apply them to past time in thought only. I also learned I couldn't change anything because that's the way it happened, and it is a part of history. I could use this information to make suggestions for someone else to make changes.

The information I read about Frick might mean something. He might be passing information to others and the captain must be involved. Since I wasn't sure, I would wait and see. The next morning, we prepared to sail. A long trip was in store for us to cross the Atlantic to Georgetown, South America. We had filled all the water containers and stowed them below; the crew was anxious to leave.

We pulled out of port and set sail with the tide. The captain gave the helmsman the direction and we are again at sea. I couldn't shake the feeling this might be my last voyage. I left the top deck and went down among the men looking for Frick.

I walked up to Qwinn and asked, "Have you seen Frick anywhere, or have you heard where he might be?"

He said, "No, sir, I haven't heard anything, and I haven't seen him anywhere." He might be on the next deck down." I went below weaving through the men that were cleaning the cannons; the others were just sitting around talking amongst themselves. I saw Dagger Dan and asked him, "Have you seen Frick?"

He said, "No, sir, I haven't." I kept looking. As I was climbing down the third deck ladder, I heard someone call out, "Mr. Pierce!"

"Mr. Pierce!" Skyler called out again. I stopped and he said, "Mr. Pierce, sir, I found out that Frick didn't board ship at port."

I thought that whatever he and the captain were up to, it was going to come to a head real soon.

It was getting late in the day and the captain said to me, "Mr. Pierce I would like you to dine with me and the junior officers this evening."

I said, "Thank you, sir. I shall be there."

Later that evening I went to the captain's quarters and the officers were standing around drinking wine and talking. The captain asked me to come in. Offering me a glass of wine, he asked, "How is my first lieutenant tonight?"

I replied, "Very well, Captain, thank you for asking."

He said, "Are all the men doing their work? Are there any problems?"

I then looked at him and said, "Everyone is fine and doing their work, except one."

He asked, "Which one would that be?" I said, "Frick."

He asked, "Frick?" I said, "Yes, sir."

"What the devil is wrong with Frick? Is he seasick?" he asked with a snort.

"No, it's just he is missing—he's not aboard." I said, "We have searched the ship top to bottom. He is not on board."

The captain looked at me and said, "I will have him punished."

I said, "He never got on board at our last port of call, sir." Then I asked the captain, "Sir, by any chance do you know anything about that?"

The captain gave me a stern look and said, "I had no idea that any of the crew had left the ship except for the two that went with me."

I said, "Yes, sir." I then excused myself. "By your leave, sir." I was tired and left for my quarters. When I got to my cabin Skyler was waiting to talk to me. We went in and he asked me, "Sir, did you find anything out about Frick?"

I said, "No, nothing. If anyone knows of his whereabouts, they are keeping it to themselves."

"Is the captain up to something?" he asked.

I told him, "I think Frick may have heard us that one evening talking about taking this ship. He may have said something to the captain. I also think that the captain may have told Frick to stay behind. He may have gone to someone in the fleet and told them what is about to happen. I'm not sure though."

Skyler then asked me, "When are we going to take the ship?" I said, "In about two or three weeks."

He said, "I don't know, sir. The men may not wait that long."

I told him, "You go and tell the others that we must wait. We will be further out to sea, and I have a plan."

Skyler said, "You know that the junior officers will most likely take the captain's side and we may have a big fight on our hands."

I said, "I know that there might be people who may get hurt and some might even die. But if we want this ship, that is the price we pay for it. Now you go tell the others to be patient."

He said, "I will tell the others to wait."

I knew what was about to happen and that many would die, but I couldn't seem to stop it, nor did I want to; this ship will be mine.

The next day the weather was fair, and sailing was good. The captain was strolling toward the bow as he approached me and he asked, "Mr. Pierce, has anyoneseen the missing manFrick?"

I said, "I believe he jumped ship and is to be considered a deserter." If caught he would be tried and hung. Then I asked the captain, "About how long will it take us to get to Georgetown?"

He said, "About two or three months, depending on the weather." According to my calculations in another month we would be at the halfway point. I went down to my quarters and got a map out to see about where that would put us. Using my compass and a sextant I figured out approximately where that would be. That put us at latitude 20° north and longitude 40° west; it would be in the middle of the Atlantic.

I went topside to check on the crew when the captain asked me, "Mr. Pierce, please go and retrieve my four-draw telescope; it is on my desk in my quarters."

I went down and entered his room. I saw his telescope and went over to pick it up when I saw the two chests. The temptation was too much. I tried the lid. Shockingly, they were unlocked. So, I opened one and then the other. One was full of small gold bars; the other one had diamonds, pearls, and ornate bejeweled necklaces. I wasn't sure what he had planned to do with them, but I knew what I would do with them.

I picked up the telescope and hurried topside. The captain took the scope and walked to the stern of the ship on the starboard side. He was looking northeast for something. One of the men in the crow's nest was looking in the same direction when he pointed and hollered, "I can see the top of a ship's mast, sir." I went over to the captain and asked him, "Captain, can you see her flag?"

He said, "No, it is too far over the horizon. I think it might be one of the fleet's ships that sailed out of the port of Las Palmas."

I asked him, "Captain, could I talk to you in your quarters, sir?"

He turned to the helmsman and told him, "I want you to hold this ship's course. You in the crow's nest, main mast, I want you to keep a weather eye out for any kind of ships." Then he turned to me and said, "Let's go."

We went to his quarters and shut the door. I asked him, "Sir, what are you doing with the two chests?"

He said, "Mr. Pierce, those are a private business deal and none of your business." I asked him, "Captain, what about Frick? Do you know where he is?"

He said, "No." I could tell that he was lying. I then asked him, "Are you expecting a ship to show up?"

He said, "No, but I was told that the French and the Spanish are also sailing this part of the Atlantic and we should be cautious."

I then heard a voice for me to wake up. Shirley told me, "Matt, you have been under for a long time. How do you feel?"

I said, "I am okay, just a little tired. I really need to talk to you, William, Dr. Beckley, and Dr. Adams." As soon as possible.

She said, "I will check my schedule before I call Dr. Beckley. You can call William after I call him."

Dr. Adams said, "My schedule is open, and I am available anytime; just let me know." When I left her office, everything was arranged.

After writing everything that happened in my last session, I called William. I needed to tell him my plans. When he answered he said, "I'm glad you called. Is everything progressing for you?" he asked.

I told him, "Yes, there is something new all the time but it's not unexpected. I need to talk to you about all that has happened as soon as possible."

He said, "I can be there shortly."

I told him, "That will be fine." I then asked him, "Will you be available in two days at nine a.m.?"

He said, "Yes, but why?"

I told him, "I will explain all of that to you in later."

William arrived, and I asked him to come in. We went into the living room and sat down. "William," I said, handing him a glass of wine, "It is good to see you."

I said, "There are a lot of things I need to say, and I want to get right into it, so here it goes." I asked him, "William, do you feel your soul has traveled through a passage in time the same way as mine has? How do you think John Pierce and Skyler Wilkes ended up here as Matthew Stein and William Breeley?"

He said, "I know that my soul traveled at the same time yours did. I'm not sure how our two souls managed to be together in some kind of time portal. Through my hypnotic sessions with Shirley, we presumed that there was some other entity that traveled with my soul in that portal. I have known this for a long time, but it took me this long to make the connection with you. I had the impression when I went through this whole process with Shirley that someone or something came with me."

He continued, "I started to put two and two together and thought by chance you might have come through with me. I watched you from afar and collected as much

information about you as I could. You are doing the same things I did. When you're reading you stare off like you're someplace else, daydreaming, etc." He said, "I have observed you do all these things and more."

"Matt, I've watched you. I went through the same thing as you're doing now. I know I have told you this before. My knowledge of the sunken vessels is not as clear as yours. That is why I approached you." He also said, "I want to preserve all that I find and give it back to the countries from which it came."

I asked him, "How did you end up with the four coins?"

He said, "You will find this out later in your sessions, but I will tell you anyway.

Matt, you are not going to believe what I am about to tell you, but here it is. I knew where we buried two small pouches of gold. Both had four coins in them. We burned our initials on them; mine was S.W. The initials on yours you will discover in future sessions." He said, "I bought mine in Barbados in a souvenir shop when I went there looking for some of the ships. I was told that a person who found them was using a metal detector. He sold them and they ended up in the souvenir shop. This happened because no one knew what they were or their value; they didn't research them. These are poor people; cash in hand is of more value to them. All they care about is that their immediate needs are being met. So, the rest is history." He chuckled at that statement, "History! Wow!"

I then told him, "I bought mine in Barbados too. I was on a field trip with a group of students." This was hard for me to understand. I couldn't believe what I was hearing. I know William felt the same way. Both of us had to accept this because of our past experiences.

I then told him why I wanted him here. I explained to him, "Will, I am not going to come back out of my next session."

He asked me, "What do you mean about not coming out of the next session? What do you plan on doing?"

I told him, "I want to stay in that time period if I can. When I die back there, I hope my soul will go wherever souls go. I don't want to travel through a passage in time."

He asked, "Is that possible? Wouldn't it change this present time and history?"

I told him, "No one knows the answer to that. I can say that with all the recordings Dr. Walker is doing along with my journal, they might make some sense out of this. I think it is necessary. I don't belong here. I must fix my history. It's like asecond chance to correct a mistake. This should never have happened. I have a letter here for you and it's not to be opened until I'm gone. William, I have a huge favor to ask. Would you take care of Buck for me?"

He said, "Matt, this is crazy. This just doesn't make any sense."

I said, "William, I have to do this. Will you take care of my dog?"

He said, "Yes, Matt, I will take good care of him, but it is still crazy."

I said, "I also have a letter here for Shirley. I would like her to write my story and have you assisted her if she has any questions. William, there is one last journal I am currently working on. Please see that Shirley gets it. She keeps the copies of my notes, videos, and audio recordings for future use. I would also like Dr. Beckley to have copies because of his interest in this topic. The university paranormal and psychology department will also receive copies. I am leaving all my personal belongings, the house, all my money in my personal accounts and the four gold coins to you for helping with all of this. I said to William, "It is hard to do this, but I need to do it. It is my honor to know you not only in this present time but also in our past."

William stood up from his chair. He was very pale. He said, "It has been an honor to know you too, sir. I understand what you are trying to carry out. However, I do not understand why you are doing this. Of course, I will do as you request."

I asked him, "Don't say anything about our conversation to anyone, especially Shirley or Dr. Beckley until after I am gone."

He said, "I won't tell anyone. I will honor your wishes."

I asked him, "Would you like to be there for my last session?" William said, "I would like to be there with you."

"I will see you at Shirley's," I said.

We shook hands and he left. The next morning, I spent most of the day getting all the legal paperwork and documents recorded. I spent some time with Buck and watched news broadcasts. I thought about my life from my childhood until now. I thought about the violence of my past life. I wondered if this was the right thing to do.

When morning came, I took Buck out early for his last walk with me. We went down to the bridge that went over the river where this whole thing started. I thought it was fitting that he and I should end it there. I looked at him and said, "Old friend, it is time to go." When we got back to the house, I loaded him in the car, and I drove him to the kennel. I gave him a hug and told him what a good friend he was. I then turned and left. I reached Shirley's office early. I wanted to complete my last journal entry.

I am Dr. Shirley Walker. My help was requested to finish this most unusual and profound story of Matthew H. Stein. This is a collaboration with Matthew's closest friend, William Breeley.

When Matthew came into my conference room, William, Dr. Beckley, Dr. Adams and I were already there. He greeted everyone and asked us to listen with no interruptions. First, he thanked us for being there. He thanked us for helping him to try to understand this most unusual story. He then asked me to write the remaining story using his journal, audio, and video recordings with the help of William Breeley.

He handed me a letter and said it was not to be opened until his death. He also instructed Dr. Adams not to try to save him if he went into heart failure. At that point he gave me a Do Not Resuscitate order that was signed and notarized. After I put him under, he said he would hopefully stay there in his own time and his soul would go where it needed to. The letters that we received would explain it all. He hoped all of us would respect his wishes. His soul needed to have peace and rest.

For a few seconds we all sat there in complete and utter silence. We were stunned by this revelation. Dr. Beckley said, "Mr. Stein, this is quite a choice you have made for yourself." He said he knew Matthew was having a tug of war with his conscience. He also knew that Matt was intent on doing this. "You are dabbling with the unknown," Dr. Beckley said. Why would you risk your life for this not knowing the outcome?

Dr. Adams quickly jumped in the conversation, agreeing with Dr. Beckley, having taken an oath to preserve life any way he could. Now Matt wanted him to disregard that oath.

Mathew replied he knew that he was dabbling with the unknown. He knew this was hard for both doctors to understand with the facts they had. He felt his soul was being pulled in two directions. He wanted to change the evil part of his past if he could. He truly felt that he must at least give it a try, whatever the outcome might be. He also spoke to Dr. Adams, saying he realized the doctor had spent his career saving people. He respected that very much. He asked that Dr. Adams respect him by not helping.

Then William stood and said, "Matt, I don't agree with this decision, but I wish you the best." He gave him a hug and shook his hand, as we all did.

Matthew told me, "William will be allowed to stay until the end of the session." He then turned to William and told him, "I will now tell you where the *Shark* is lying. Please save it from looters. William, I want you to know that this place is only in my memory, but I know it is a real. It is southeast of Palm Island, about two to three miles offshore at 12° north, 61° west in about one hundred feet of water. Trust me, I know the *Shark* is in that vicinity.

He then said, "Okay, I am ready. I will tell you everything that is going on."

"Matthew," I said, "in your last session you left off in the captain's quarters. You were talking to him about the French and Spanish ships in the area where the *Intrepid* was sailing."

Pierce told the captain, "Sir, I feel the men need to have some practice on the guns."

The captain looked at him and said, "That's a good idea but you may not want to shoot live powder but to just dry practice."

Pierce said, "Aye, sir, I will get right to it." He saluted the captain and went topside. He approached Skyler and told him, "I want you to gather the men because I want to talk to them." When they were all there, he told them, "Men, we are to have gunnery practice in one hour. You are to get things ready. It will be dry runs only, no live fire, and be quick about it." After everyone was excused, they went on to prepare for the training.

Skyler came up to Pierce and asked him, "Sir, are you feeling ill? You look a little peaked."

Pierce told him he had a great lack of trust in the captain. He felt that the captain was lying about Frick's disappearance and he thought that Frick was giving information to the authorities about the upcoming mutiny. Plus, he felt they were being followed.

Pierce told Skyler, "Do not tell this to anyone because the crew might do something. That would not be good, and it will ruin the plans." He told Skyler, "I want you to keep your ears open to any information about Frick. If you hear anything, I want you to bring it to me right away." About an hour went by and Pierce ordered all hands to battle stations and the practices were going well. The captain, however, was not watching; he was looking through the telescope for something. Pierce went up to him, gave him his report, and told him the practice went well. The captain said, "That is good. Now go secure all guns and hatches."

Pierce again asked, "Captain, is there a problem? What are you looking for?"

The captain told him, "You are to go about your duties, sir. You are to make sure the men are doing their work. I will take care of the ship." The captain then looked up to the crow's nest and asked the lookout if he saw anything.

The lookout said, "I see nothing Sir."

The captain told him, "I want you to keep a weather eye out for anything and to report it right away."

I asked Matthew, "Where are you on the ocean?"

He said, "I'm not sure, maybe close to the halfway point. The sailing weather has been very good so far, though." He then said, "I think that there is some trouble starting."

Skyler approached Pierce and said, "Mr. Pierce Sir, the men are getting restless they want to know when we will take over the ship."

Pierce told Skyler, "I'm sure that we should be halfway; we will be taking her today." He then said, "Skyler, I want you to get some of the men on the weapons deck and some on the main deck. I will call the captain up from his quarters." Pierce told Skyler, "There will be some of the officers who will have to be tied and gagged. They will not be killed. Just be quick and quiet about it." Pierce said, "Skyler, you are to let me know when everyone is in place before I call the captain." Skyler went about the ship and told everyone what the plans were and set everyone to their places. Skyler then told Pierce, "Sir, everyone is ready and waiting for your orders." Pierce called the captain up to the main deck. When he got there, he saw all the crew standing there with Pierce in the middle of them. He asked, "Mr. Pierce what is going on here? Why aren't the men working?"

Pierce said to him, "You know what is happening: we are taking over the ship." The captain drew his pistol but was quickly subdued. Pierce told the officers, "Anyone of you who wants to join us can stay. But if not, you will go with the captain." There were eight officers on board and four stood by the Captain.

The captain asked, "Pierce, what do you have planned for me and my fellow officers?"

Pierce told him, "You are going to be set adrift and given food and water for one month for five people." Pierce ordered, "Now take them and put them into a lifeboat along with their provisions and cast them off."

The captain told him, "Pierce, you are a bloody coward; you are lower than the deepest pit of Hell. You are scurvy scum. No one takes my ship from me. I swear I will come after you. You will be caught and hung for treason. I swear this, Pierce, you will be hung along with everyone here. Take heed all of you, take heed!" When the captain was pushed off, Pierce turned to the crew and said, "Set full sail towards Georgetown."

That evening when things calmed down Pierce told Skyler, Qwinn, Dan, and Tom to meet him in the captain's quarters. When they arrived

Pierce told them, "I am making Skyler here my first mate. The rest of you will oversee the other areas set by Skyler." He then said, "I am going to change my name. My new name is going to be Captain Rue. That is how I want everyone to address me from now on. The name of this ship needs to be changed too. I am going to leave that up to the crew. They are to pick its name and to have it to me tomorrow morning."

The next morning the crew were waiting for Captain Rue to come topside. When he did the men gave him a Huzzah. Qwinn approached him, saluted, and said, "We have a name for the ship, sir."

Rue said, "Before you tell me the name of the ship, I want all of you to remember that I am the captain of this ship. However, since we are no longer in the service of His Majesty, you will follow my orders but there will be no saluting. You will call me captain or sir. I want to be respected and you will get respect from me. Is that clear?"

They all said, "Yes, sir, we understand."

Then he asked them, "What name do you have for the ship?" Qwinn said, 'We want to call it the *Shark.*"

Rue told them, "All of you will receive a reward for your loyalty." He then gave the order, "Skyler, I want you to remove all of the nameplates and plaques that have the ship's name on them. You are to stow them and keep them for future use. We might be able to use them as a decoy." Rue then said, "Qwinn, I want you to put the best man up in the crow's nest to keep a sharp eye out for any ships." He also told him, "I want you to keep all swords, guns, and powder locked up. When that's done, bring the keys to me."

Skyler asked, "Captain what about the flag? What should we do with the one we are flying?"

Rue told him, "I want it to be taken down fold it and keep it. You know it might come in handy later on." He said whatever the crew wanted for a flag was fine with him but not to fly it until he ordered them to do so.

That afternoon Rue was charting the ports they were to stop at when Skyler knocked on his door. Rue told him, "Yes, yes come in."

Skyler asked, "Captain, how do you feel? Are you ill?"

Rue said, "I am fine. I am charting our course and ports that we are to travel to.

But I am wondering if what we have done is the right thing."

Skyler explained to him, "Captain, you know if you didn't do it the crew would have done it anyway. I am sorry about all of this falling on your shoulders, but things could have turned out worse than they did."

Rue agreed and told Skyler where they were headed. "We are going to Georgetown and will do our trading before the fleet gets word of our mutiny. We will be trading for gold and silver. This will be split with the crew after we buy fresh food and supplies." Rue also told Skyler, "The men can have shore leave too. No one is to say anything about this ship. If they do, they will be shot make sure they all know this."

Matthew told me, "I can still feel a huge tug of war on in my soul about staying here and not returning to the present day."

Dr. Beckley asked, "Matt, do you think all of these things you see seem real at the moment?"

Matt said, "Yes, but I have no control of my destiny yet. I feel I have to fulfill my quest. I have to keep going."

While Rue was still in his chambers, he sat mulling over his new role as captain. He was also pondering what might happen in any of the ports they would enter. He knew that they wouldn't be flying a flag so there might be trouble. He called Skyler down to talk to him. Rue told him, "We will have to fly the British flag so no one will suspect us. It might keep us from having any problems." He also told him, "If anyone asks, we will tell them the captain is not feeling well. He is staying in his cabin. We are going to have to put up the ship's old nameplates for a little while. We have to mount them so we can remove them anytime."

Skyler said, "Aye, sir. I will get right on it and tell the carpenter."

Rue also said, "Skyler, we will be sailing to the Grenadine Islands after Georgetown. The crew can take some shore leave there for a while. I feel as though the men need some free time to themselves." Just as Skyler was leaving Rue told him, "I really need to get some rest. Wake me if any ship or land is spotted."

Matthew told us, "I think there is some time that has gone by somehow. I'm not sure but it may have been about two weeks or more. I know this because we were in the middle of the Atlantic and now the man in the crow's nest has spotted land."

Skyler came down to wake Rue and told him, "Sir, land has been spotted." Rue got the map out and looked at the coordinates to see if it was Guyana. That is where they were supposed to be. He then ran upstairs and checked with the helmsman, Georgetown, Guyana straight ahead.

He asked Skyler, "Did the carpenter get all of the nameplates on and is the flag in place?"

Skyler said, "Captain, everyone is aware of what is going to happen. They are to act like British sailors in port. Yes, everything is in place."

Rue said, "That's good, once we have done all of our trading and loading the supplies, we will leave Georgetown right away."

Skyler asked him, "What about the men, sir? They would like to have some shore leave."

Rue told him, "Yes, they can have at least four hours. They are to be back on board and on time. If they agree to that, I will give them some gold to spend."

Skyler said, "I will go tell them and I will report back with their answer."

Rue told Skyler, "No, never mind. I will tell them myself." They went topside and called the crew together. Rue told them, "Men, while we are in port, I feel you should have some shore leave. It can only be about four hours. If anyone mentions anything about a mutiny, they will be shot." He also told them what he expected from them and that if they followed his orders, he would give them some gold to spend. They all understood and agreed to his terms. Rue told the men, "I want all of you to get the ship ready to go into port. We will enter early in the morning and leave late that night."

The next day was rainy when the ship entered Georgetown. There were other ships there, but the *Shark* docked away from them further down the pier. There were some native people there to talk to the captain. Rue told them, "Come aboard."

The crew started to unload the goods that were to be traded. Rue had made adeal with the natives to trade some wine and a little ivory for their gold. After this exchange

Rue told Skyler that he was to go with him to a port warehouse. This is the warehouse where Captain Phipps said they are to pick up the gold bars. The bars were painted over with gray paint so no one else would know what they were. The gray paint would hide the gold and blend in with the lead bars that were to be picked up also. When they arrived at the warehouse Rue talked to an unidentified man. They talked for a minute, then shook hands. When they returned to the ship Rue told Skyler to scratch the bars before they loaded them to make sure they were gold and not lead. Following Captain Phipps's directions, they put the gold in one section and the lead in the aft compartment. The rest of the ivory and wine would be unloaded and given to thewarehousemen.

Two sailors from another British ship came walking by. They stopped and asked the crew if they could talk to Captain Phipps because they knew him well. Skyler approached and said, "You can't see the captain, for he is ill. However, you can talk to First Officer Pierce if you wish."

The two sailors said, "No, that it is fine. We will leave for now and see him later." They continued down the pier.

Rue then told the men, "We have to hurry and keep loading the ship. The men were simultaneously stocking the ship with fresh water and food supplies. They hurried because it had to be finished by that afternoon. Rue told the men, "Now you are to go enjoy yourselves and to be back by ten bells." Then he gave each man six gold coins to spend.

Rue then went below and left the three men that did not want shore to leave to guard the ship.

Rue was below trying to figure out his next stop when Qwinn and Skyler knocked on his door. Rue told them to enter. Qwinn said, "Sir, the two sailors who were here earlier are back. They want to see Phipps."

Rue stood and asked, "Are all of the men back yet?" Skyler said, "No, sir."

Rue told them, "Shore leave is cancelled. Bring back every man. I will talk to the two sailors." When they reached topside the two men were standing on board. Rue asked them, "Who told you that you could come aboard?"

One of them said, "No one, sir. We just came aboard."

Rue told them, "Gentlemen, may I remind you that you need permission from the captain or officer in command to board a ship. You are not to set foot on it until then. I will also remind you I can bring you up on charges for boarding without permission. So, state your business here and be quick about it."

One of them said, "We beg your pardon, sir. We ask your forgiveness. We ask if we could only see the captain for a moment, sir."

Rue told them, "I think you may have misunderstood me when I said no., I will explain to you again, gentlemen. The Captain is ill and not to be disturbed." He then said, "The business you have here is concluded, so may I ask you to leave?" As he escorted them off the ship, he turned and told the three men on guard to start preparations to get under way. Skyler and Qwinn showed up with the crew, and most of them were not happy. Rue told them, "Men, we are being watched. We have had British soldiers here at the ship looking for Captain Phipps. I feel if they figure everything out then we could be captured. You will have your leave at our next port of call. We need to leave the harbor at once. Mr. Wilkes let us get under way. They soon proceeded out of port and went offshore about five miles and anchored. Rue told the men to finish getting the cargo prepared for a long voyage. He would look for another port to continue their leave. He decided to head for New Amsterdam and put into port there. He thought that the men could spend a couple of days there and not have to worry about any British ships.

The next morning the men were talking among themselves and questioning the way Rue was running the ship. Rue gathered all the men together on the main deck. He told them, "Men, I told you why we needed to leave. We were very close to getting caught. If the two sailors that were friends of Phipps didn't believe our story of his illness they may have come back with more men. I did not want them to return. The best thing to do was to leave port and go somewhere else." He then told them, "I found a small port just south from where we are. You men can spend a couple of days there." Rue said, "Men, you came to me to command this ship. You told me that you wanted Phipps out and me in. I told you my rules and you agreed to them. Right?" They all said, "Aye, Captain."

Rue then said, "Now if any one of you is not happy about my command and my decisions you better speak now or hold your tongue. Now are you with me or against me?" They all said, "With you, sir!" He then ordered, "All right now, set sail with full canvas." He then gave the directions to the helmsman. Skyler asked the captain, "Sir, where are the sails set for?" Rue told him, "To New Amsterdam. We should arrive there late tonight."

When they left, they had a good wind as they headed south. The man in the crow's nest spotted land along with the person at the bow watch. Captain Rue told the helmsman to sail up the river about five miles or more. "There will be a port on our left that will be New Amsterdam," he told him.

Captain Rue told the crew they could have two days leave at New Amsterdam. If anyone was not back on the ship on time, he would be left behind.

Rue told Skyler, "I want you to keep an eye on the men. You make sure all of them come back." He also told him, "I want you to take Qwinn with you. You are to be in charge until I come back to the ship."

Skyler asked him, "Where are you going?"

Rue told him, "I am going to make a deal on some gold for myself."

Two days went by and Rue was standing on the upper deck when all the men returned. It was in the morning sometime, and the men were in very good spirits. It had been a good leave for them.

Captain Rue had made his gold deals. He had three small chests put in his quarters. The men reported on board and Rue ordered to set sail.

Skyler asked the captain "Sir, where are we bound?"

Rue said to him, "We are going to sail northwest to the Grenadine Islands. There is a small island there called Barbados. There we will take on fresh water and fruit. We will also relax, clean the ship, and make repairs if we need too." Rue thought it would take about three or four days to get there.

Skyler said to him, "Captain, do you think this area might be too dangerous? You know a lot of British ships sail through there."

Rue told him, "Yes, but we will fly the British flag while we are at sea to throw them off." Rue then said, "Skyler, I want you and Qwinn to have the men go through dry battle runs. This is so everyone will know what they are doing. If we come across any French or Spanish ships, we will attack them. We will send them to the bottom after we collect all of their goods, gold, and silver." They set sail for Barbados and it was about two or three days later when Tom, who was in the crow's nest, spotted land.

They lowered the anchor about two miles offshore on the southeast side of the island. There was a beach and a small cove nearby. It looked like a good place to rest and relax. The men lowered a skiff and took some water barrels with them. Captain Rue took Skyler aside. He told him he wanted to talk to him about something personal. They went down to Rue's quarters and he told him to sit down.

He said, "Skyler, I have here two pouches that have four gold coins in each pouch. I had our initials burned on them and covered in wax to protect the leather. We are going ashore to bury them in a special place.

We will be the only ones who will know where they are." Skyler asked, "Why are we doing this?" Rue told him, "This is just in case something might happen to either one of us. We will always be able to come back to dig it up and have a little gold to start over with."

Skyler then asked him, "Why the two pouches? Why not just one?"

Rue explained to him, "If we both come here at the same time, each of us will have a pouch. The pouches only have four coins in them. This will be enough to get started. If you have more than that, greed will be upon you."

Skyler then said, "I might dig them both up and take all the gold."

Rue said, "Yes, you could do that, but I burned our initials into the leather. If only one of us comes to dig his up, he then will dig up the other one to see if it is there or not. This will tell us if the other one is dead or alive. If the other pouch is there it is to be reburied just in case the other may return one day. If one of us returns and they are both gone there will be the pirate's death curse upon his life's soul. Would you want the curse or four gold coins? You have to make that choice." Rue then said, "If you agree to this, we will make a blood pact to our friendship to activate the curse." They both agreed and then as they held one coin, they cut their palms and shook on it to seal the pact.

When Matthew was telling this part of the story I looked over at William and watched him reach inside of his coat and pull out a little leather pouch. I could see some burn marks on it like lettering, but it was very faint. He then showed us the four gold coins that they buried centuries before. We were all shocked.

Matt said, "Skyler and I came up on deck climbed down to a lifeboat to go ashore.

When we got to the shore, I could feel how warm it was. It feels good to walk on land again."

Captain Rue and Skyler buried their pouches and went to help the others to collect the ship's water and fruit.

That evening Rue was in his quarters having dinner and charting his next port of call when he heard someone call out, "Ahoy there, it be a ship on the horizon." Rue grabbed his telescope and hurried topside. Everyone crowded the starboard side of the ship as Rue looked through the telescope. Rue said, "I can't see a flag because it is too dark. Men put all the lights out. There is to be no noise until the ship has passed. Look, there is no moon so there is a good chance we won't be spotted. I want to have all guns at the ready. Everyone is to be alert and standing by when needed." He told the men, "I want you to pair up at each gun site. Every other man will sleep in four-hour shifts until daylight. I want every man awake to stay alert and make no noise." The ship passed them by several hours later as the sun started to come up.

Rue gathered all the men together and said, "I could see the ship's flag and name just before it passed us by. He told them, "It is a Spanish ship. It looked as though she is sailing heavy. Her name is *La Flora Cruz*. I have heard of this ship. She is a cargo vessel that transports goods and gold to ports in the Caribbean. She doesn't have a lot of guns, but she does have speed. Do you want to catch her?" He asked. "Aye, Captain," they said. Rue then asked them, "Do you want to take her as a prize or send her to the bottom?" The crew said, "We want to send her down, but we want her cargo first."

Rue told them, "Hoist anchor. Set full canvas and run up the colors." They left Barbados in a chase to catch the *La Flora Cruz*. They finally caught her halfway between Barbados and the island of Tobago. The *Shark* came up behind her. When they were within firing range Rue ordered the crew to open fire from the two bow cannons. One hit through the other ship's rear windows, which blew out part of its stern. The other one missed. Rue told the men to try to hit either her keel or her back mast to slow her down. Two more shots hit the keel wheel. That killed the helmsman. They also hit an outrigger mast. Skyler hollered for everyone to get down on the deck. The *La Flora Cruz* fired back with three cannons. The *Shark* was hit all three times, once in the forward cargo area. Rue ordered the men to pull up on her port side and fire all cannons when theylined up with her. The *Shark* was a lot faster because it was not weighted down. It pulled alongside the *La Flora Cruz* about fifty yards off and cut loose with all guns. They knocked out several of their guns and hit the forward mast. The men went below to get guns, knives, and swords, they also got the grappling hooks. They pulled ahead of the *Cruz* and circled around her and then went to her starboard side. The *Shark* fired again, and her crew could hear the screaming of the dying men on the other ship. Rue couldalso hear the clashing of metal against metal and see swords hitting each other. He could see the men losing their lives. Skyler boarded the *Cruz* along with several men. Rue stayed on board the *Shark* along with

Qwinn and about half the crew. The *Cruz* was not ready for a battle. Her crew gave up early because her captain was killed. Their first officer offered to hand over the captain's sword. Rue then came over to accept their surrender.

Some of the men from the *Shark* told Rue that there were a lot of trade goods along with gold and silver. Rue ordered the men to start transferring all her cargo to the *Shark*.

Qwinn asked, "What should we do with their crew that is still alive?" Rue told him, "I want to talk to them for a minute." He asked, "Is there anyone here who can speak English?"

One man spoke up and said, "Sir, I can a little bit." Rue said to him, "If any of you want to join us you can start loading our ship. If not, you will be put into lifeboats and set adrift with hardtack and water. Now tell them what I just told you." About fifteen men joined the crew, even the one that spoke English.

Skyler came topside about this time and told Rue, "The gold and silver is not only in coins but candelabras, cups, goblets, and silver utensils." He then told Rue, "Sir, you know that the Shark can't haul all of this cargo. We have no space and there's too much weight."

Rue asked, "Skyler, what are the coins in?"

"They are in chests with small bars of gold and silver," Skyler said.

Rue told him, "I want you to take just the chests and bars. Leave the rest."

Matt told us they took almost everything, including the weapons and gunpowder.

He also told us he set a powder charge with a fuse to be lit just before they left.

Matt told us the *Shark* was damaged. Rue had lost seven men in the battle. Two of them were Dagger Dan and Toothless Tom.

William spoke up. "I can remember that battle. I feel a lot of sorrow about losing my friends." I then asked him, "Will, are you doing okay?"

He said he was fine. But he had that faraway look in his eyes. I felt he still had that sorrow deep inside for the friends he once had centuries ago.

Everything was brought aboard that they could save and was not too heavy. The order was given to light the fuse as they sailed away from her quickly. Matt said that he just wanted to put a big hole in the bottom of the ship. This was because he did not want a lot of debris floating around.

He told us that they are about a quarter of a mile away when it blew and then went down. He also told us that they had to make some minor repairs to his ship. This could be done at sea. They would set course to St. Lucia Island for any major repairs.

Rue told Skyler, "See to the injured men. Then give me a casualty list."

"Where are we to set sail for?" Skyler asked. Rue told him, "We are going to go to the port of Castries on the island of St Lucia. We will make our major repairs there. I will give the men some money so they can enjoy themselves."

Rue told the men to keep working and to look out for ships on the horizon. He told the crow's nest to keep a sharp eye out for ships and land. It wasn't too long before the man in the crow's nest spotted land on both sides of the ship. Rue told the helmsman to steer north by west. He was to go around the island on the starboard side of the ship. The port they were going to was north of the island. In a large inlet to the bay was a big port with all kinds of shipping.

When they arrived, there were all sorts of ships coming and going. They had to be careful how they entered the port. Rue told the helmsman, "I want you to keep the port on the starboard side. We will dock on that side of the bay." He told the helmsman to dock at Seraphine. From there they could travel to the villages and rest for a while. After docking the ship Rue gathered the men. He told them, "Men, you know not to talk about the ship. But I want you to have a good time. Don't get into any trouble." He also said, "There has to be four of you at a time on board to watch the ship." He told them, "There is no one that can come aboard unless they are part of the crew." Each man had to report back in eight hours and that's when they would switch guards. Rue gave each man some gold when they left. He stayed aboard to chart the next sailing route. He also wanted to assess the ship's damage to make repairs.

I was feeling that Matthew and Captain Rue were starting to merge somehow because Matt was talking very low. He was talking to himself or slipping back into that time where he came from. There were times I had to ask him to speak up, but it was becoming more frequent as time progressed. Dr. Beckley and Dr. Adams concurred with me. I wanted to wake him, but William said not to because this was what Matthew wanted.

I asked Matt, "What is Rue's plan now?" He said, "We are going to sail to a chain of islands. I need to find a good place to hide for a while.

I'm looking for a cove or some small bay." He told us, "It is getting dark and the men are back. He then went topside to watch the lanterns being lit. The evening air is filling with men's cheers along with laughter and gayety. A lot of drinking is going on in the port's village.

"There is some gun fire, women laughing, drunken sailors walking by the ship. Rue ordered three men to pull the catwalk up so no one could come aboard or leave. As the night went on the partying died down. A quiet hush fell over the port." Matt said, "I am still on the upper deck listening to the faint sounds in the harbor. Occasionally I can hear a cat or dog. But mostly I hear the small waves splash against the ship." Matt said, "I can feel more and more of Captain Rue's soul. I just want to sail to be able to go without any plans, just go."

The next day Rue ordered the men to start the repairs. He wanted them to clean and paint the areas where it was needed. He told Skyler, "I want you to check the gunpowder to see if it is still dry. Make sure that all the weapons are clean." Rue told Qwinn, "I want you to check all the food and water to make sure it hasn't gone bad."

That evening a British ship came in and docked on the other side of the harbor.

Rue brought up the telescope and saw it is a class two warship with about ninety guns. He was not able to see her name but was concerned about it being there. He told his crew, "Go to town; have a good time. I want you back here in four hours because we might have to leave here sooner than I thought." That night when the crew was gone Rue with two other crewmen took the nameplates off the ship. This was just in case someone spotted her.

When the men came back, two of them wanted to talk to the captain about something important. Rue told them, "Go to my quarters but have Skyler andQwinn come too." When Rue reached his room, he entered and asked them, "What is so important?"

They told him, "We were having a bit of rum when these three sailors from the British ship came in. They started to talk a might too much. They told us they picked up a lifeboat that was set adrift with five sailors. It seems now there is a captain with four officers. Two of the officers died so they buried them at sea. The other three were near death. The surviving captain said he is going to get the man responsible and hang the entire crew. They also told us that the captain of their ship took them back to the Canary Islands to get them well."

Qwinn asked, "Did you hear of any names that might have been mentioned?" They said, "No. But they did say that there was a man who jumped that ship while they were in port at Las Palmas." Skyler asked them if the sailors had mentioned the name of the man who jumped ship. One of them said, "I did hear it. His name is kind of odd. I think his name is Frick." The other said, "Aye, which is his name. They told us about how he had gone to prison."

Qwinn said, "I hope he dies there."

Rue said, "He is the one who was giving all the information to Phipps and probably to the admiral." Rue turned and looked across the bay. He said, "The ship that came in must have Captain Phipps on board. If it does, he will recognize the *Shark* as the *Intrepid*." He told the crew, "We must leave tonight. I'm not going to get caught inside the bay. We will anchor outside the inlet until morning."

Rue ordered all the men to get the ship ready to sail. Late that night they left the pier. They sailed out of the bay and dropped anchor about a mile north. He told Skyler, "I want you to pick three men to keep watch. The rest of the crew is to get some sleep." He told them that they would be going to full sail in the morning.

Rue went to his quarters to make plans for the escape. They would sail north up around the island. They would then come down on the east side and head for St. George's on the island of Grenada." They would then go to the Caribbean Sea to try to hide somewhere around Jamaica. But at St. George's he could restock there.

When they were putting up the last sail one of the crew spotted a ship coming out of the bay at Castries. Rue ordered, "Pull anchor set full sail." He told the helmsman, "I want you to steer north and go around the island." Rue looked back with his telescope to see if the other ship turned to follow them. Rue told the men, "We are being followed.

Quickly set full sail." When they reached the northern point of the island, he told the helmsman, "I want you to go around and head south to St. George's." As they were making the turn, Rue looked back and saw that the other ship was falling further behind. He figured that the *Shark* could lose them quickly because it was lighter and smaller and much faster. Rue ordered the men to make sure the cannons and rifles were ready and to have all swords and knives unlocked just in case they may need them. That afternoon as they were going past St. Lucia at the southern tip Rue looked back to see if the other ship was following them. The man in the crow's nest hollered down that there was a sail off their starboard side several miles away. Rue ordered two front quarter sails at full canvas and then told the helmsman to sail straight and true. They were between two islands when Rue told the helmsman, "I want you to maintain this course."

The sailor in the crow's nest said, "Sir, there is another island coming up." Rue said, "We are to sail by it; keep this heading." Skyler asked Rue, "Captain, what is your plan?" Rue told him, "I want to get into the chain of islands that are coming up. I figure we can lose them there. Then we can sail to the Caribbean Sea from St. George's." He also told him, "Skyler, if we stand to fight them the *Shark* will lose. This ship is too small in fire power. We are outgunned and don't not have enough men."

Qwinn came up to Skyler and Rue and said, "Captain, the men want to know what the plan is."

Rue told him, "I want you to gather everyone on the main deck. I will explain to them what the plans are." When everyone was assembled Rue explained to them what was going on. He then said, "If anyone has a better idea, speak up." No one did. Rue then told them, "I hope I can get us out of this mess. If everyone follows my orders and does what I say, we might make it. If not, we will stand and fight to the end." They all agreed to the plan.

Rue then ordered the skull and crossbones to be hoisted and the *Shark* nameplates to be put back on. They were passing by St. Vincent Island at the south end. The crow's- nest spotted a ship through a passage between the two islands. Rue ordered the

helmsman, "I want you to sail between that set of small islands. You are to keep the biggest island on our starboard side. We need to stay in the middle of each channel." He then ordered the bow sails in with all the rest at half canvas. A man was throwing a knotted rope and calling out the depth. Captain Rue wanted to get a look at the ship that was following them. When they got past the smaller islands, they could see the ship well through their telescopes. It was a big British battleship, but he could not make out the name of it. Rue ordered the helmsman to turn southeast and then straight south. Rue told the men there was another group of islands where they might have a good chance of losing the bigger ship.

It was getting dark when Rue ordered the helmsman to head for a tiny island.

They were to break sail and anchor there. They would continue in the morning.

It was a moonless night, so it was very dark. The seas were calm, and the weather was warm. A silence came over ship. There was no movement on board.

I have never seen Matt more relaxed than I did at this time. During this whole ordeal he knew what was coming. I know he was looking forward to it, his destiny!

Rue told Skyler along with Qwinn to join him in his quarters. Rue wanted to get some ideas from them. But first he told everyone to keep a sharp eye and ear open for any movement on the water. He also ordered all lanterns be put out. Skyler passed the word to the men. He also told them they needed to get something to eat and drink but stay low on the main deck. Rue, Skyler and Qwinn then went below.

Qwinn asked Rue, "Captain, do you think we can outrun them? Rue looked at him then said, "No."

Skyler then asked, "Captain, what is your plan then? If we cannot outrun them and we are not strong enough to beat them in a toe-to-toe battle, then we are alldoomed." Rue told them, "Men, I feel if we can get them into the open sea, we will have a better chance to lose them with our speed. It must be in the Caribbean, not the Atlantic. The Caribbean Sea is calmer." He also told them, "I know the water there better than here. Men, you know if we are caught before we get there it could be the end of us." Qwinn spoke up and said, "Sir, no matter what happens the men are behind you. Captain, the men will fight to the end."

Rue told them they would continue south. They would sail between and around this small chain of islands until they came to the main channel, which would take them to the Caribbean." Rue then told them to get their rest there's early bells in themorning.

The next day all hands were called on deck were told to set sail south. Rue told the helmsman to go in between the small islands and to stay on the east side. The lookout in the crow's nest was ready and reported no ship in sight. They passed one big island and then a bunch of smaller ones. They were in between some small Islands when the man in the crow's nest hollered down that there was a ship coming straight at them on the starboard side. Rue ordered the helmsman to steer straight toward a small island and stay on the open-water side.

Matt's heart rate was rising, and Dr. Adams said, "We need to quit because he might die." William told him, "You will not stop him. Let him continue."

I calmed him down as much as possible and then asked him, "Matt what happened next?" Matt said, "The ship is getting closer. We are nearing a small island that is off the coast of Union Island. Rue ordered the ship to go around it, not between thetwo islands. This is because of the fear they might get boxed in and would not be able to get out. When the *Shark* made its turn, however, more of the ship was exposed. That's when the British fired and hit the main mast, killing several men.

Matt was really breathing hard, his pulse rate getting higher. I asked him if he was all right. He said he turned the ship and had the men at the ready. They fired the port side cannons and hit the British ship. Matt then said he could see a man standing on the upper deck of the ship. He said it was Captain Phipps. The British returned fire, hitting the *Shark* everywhere. They fired rifles, wounding and killing men. Rue called out for more cannon fire, and then about that time a second bank of guns from the British fired. They hit the *Shark* at midlevel. Qwinn rushed up from down below. He said they were taking on water and could not stop it.

Matt said the British fired their rifles again. Then he saw Qwinn go down with a ball striking him in the neck. He said he was looking for Skyler as they were being boarded. Sword fighting ensued and pistol fire broke out to repel the British. There were too many of them; the ship is going down. We heard Matt say, "Keep fighting, men." I noticed as did Dr. Adams that Matt's voice was growing weaker with each breath he took. It was getting harder to hear him. Dr. Adams and I walked over to him. The doctor was taking his pulse when he turned to look at me. He shook his head. I could tell by the look in the doctor's eye that Matt was failing.

Matt said in a barely audible breath as he grasped the side of the bed, "I am drawing my sword. I'm swinging it back and forth, slashing and cutting." He arched his back and in one final, barely audible breath said, "Skyler." He then collapsed in a lifeless state. Matthew H. Stein had passed away. The doctor covered Matthew as we all sat in utter silence and disbelief. I couldn't hold back my tears any longer and had to leave the room. William walked over to Matthew's lifeless body and quietly said, 'Thank you for being my friend. I hope you made it, Matt. May your soul rest in peace." William also had shed tears of sorrow for a very unique man.

That day we all parted and went our separate ways. William went off to find the *Shark*. I resumed my practice as did Dr. Adams and Dr. Beckley.

It had been six months since I had seen or heard of William. Then one sunny day in June he walked into my office. He said, "Shirley, I am very happy to see you. How have you been?"

I was very thrilled to see him and gave him a hug. He said, "Shirley, I wrote down the rest of the story of Matt's past life. This is Matt's and my connection on that fatal day," he said as he handed me an envelope.

William told me, "I never got to this point with you when I went through these sessions years ago. This is what happened to the best of his memory. You can now finish Matthew's story." After Will left I sat down to read the end of two men's lives, how they became friends now and how they were friends over two hundred years ago. A unique story of one lost soul and how his friend came with him through a passage in time.

Rue fell on the helm's deck by a gunshot wound to the chest. I, Skyler Wilkes, also fell at that same moment by a gunshot in the back. As I lay there, I looked at Captain Rue and he at me. I then rolled to one side and saw Captain Phipps standing by the rail on the British ship. I still had a pistol in my hand. With all my strength I took aim and shot him in the belly. I saw him fall and so did Captain Rue. That is all I remember. That's when I think our souls were intertwined in some kind of time passage. The *Shark* went down off the coast of a little island that only the people who live around there know, Palm Island. Signed by WILLIAM BREELEY.

It has been almost a year since Matt's passing. William and I have kept in contact.

I see him often walking Buck down by the river or in the park where Matthew would watch him chase the squirrels. He was sitting in the park doing just that one day as I sat next to him. He said, "I now know why Matt liked coming here with Buck. He is fun to watch but most of all his spirit is free, not trapped like Matt's was."

I said, "I know, Will. Hopefully someday ours will be free too." William asked me, "Can we meet to talk about some things?"

I said, "It would be nice to do that. We can meet at my office in an hour if that is all right with you."

He said, "That would be great."

When William showed up at my office, he came in and I gave him a hug. I then asked him, "How was your day withBuck?"

He said, "Very enjoyable as always."

I then told him to have a seat and then asked him, "What's on your mind?" He asked me, "Do you think Matt's soul really moved on?"

I told him, "I don't know. No one will ever know what happens to their soul until they die. That is left up to a higher power."

I asked him, "Why do you want to know, William?"

He said, "It is a question that we all ask sometime in our lives. I thought that maybe you might have the answer."

I said, "No, William, I don't. However, there is the Holy spirit waiting for you to ask that question if you believe. He is there for you anytime."

He told me, "I located the *Shark* with the gold and silver still aboard. I also found something else there. This is really bizarre."

I asked him, "What is it you have found?"

He told me, "There was a wax-sealed letter inside one of the coin chests." I asked him, "What did it say?"

He reached into his pocket pulled it out to let me read it.

All it said was, "William and Shirley, Thank you." It is dated 1720.

I, Shirley Walker, fulfilled Matthew H. Stein's requests. I have often thought about whether his soul was set free. I'm sure it was. He will be missed.

I, William Breeley, only hope that my friend Matthew was set free. To the people who read this story, may you think about the possibilities.